Carver's Box

A novel by

John M. Hutchinson

illustrations by

Robert Little

Illustrations by Robert Little

Published by Kids Book Press Publishing,
an imprint of A & S Publishing, A & S Holmes. Inc.
Sharon Kizziah-Holmes – Publishing Coordinator
Springfield, MO

ISBN 10: 1-945669-34-9
ISBN 13: 978-1-945669-34-7

DEDICATION

For My Grandson, Flint.

PART ONE

ONE

What's in a Name?

She stood on the crumbling walkway, a foot from the bottom step of the porch. She shielded her squinting eyes from the sun by the arc of her tiny palm.

"What's your name?" she asked.

"Duncan Sheets, at your service," he said with a deep bow. "What's yours?"

"I'm Tina Ng."

"Ng... that's not a name. It's a sound."

"Oh yeah! Well, it's my name... so there. And what about Duncan Sheets? Sounds like something you do at a laundromat. Dunk Sheets. Dunk Sheets. Talk about a dumb name."

The boy at the top of the stairs looked at his sticklike visitor for several long seconds before breaking into a wide grin. "That's pretty funny," he said. "Dunk Sheets. Laundromat. I must remember that."

She pursed her lips but said nothing.

"My mom made some Kool Aid and we have Oreos. Want some?" Duncan asked, his voice now softer, more inviting.

"Why would I want any of your dumb Kool Aid?"

"It's not *my* dumb Kool Aid. It's my mom's, and it's lime.

Oreos are double-stuffed. Sure you don't want some?"

She glared at him, her skinny brown arms crossed over her chest and wrapped around her body.

The boy at the top of the stairs looked at his sticklike visitor.

"Well, if it's *lime* Kool Aid and the Oreos are *double*-stuffed… okay. But I only like *lime* Kool Aid. Single-stuffed Oreos are dumb."

"Come on up then."

Tina hesitated, as if changing her mind, before stomping up the stairs. She brushed past Duncan and strode through the torn screen door into the dark and musty hallway.

Just then, Mrs. Sheets peered around the far end of the hallway. "Well, hello," she said. "Whom do I have the pleasure of meeting?"

"I'm Tina Ng. And my name is *not* a sound; it's a Cantonese name. It means five."

Mrs. Sheets glanced at her son Duncan and suppressed a tiny smile as if to ask, *my, my, what have we here?*

This exchange between mother and son did not escape Tina Ng, whose face morphed into a pugnacious little scowl. But she said nothing.

With a quick recovery, Mrs. Sheets led the children to a worn oak table topped with fresh yellow place mats. As Duncan and Tina eased into wobbly oak chairs, Mrs. Sheets retrieved the pitcher of lime Kool Aid and two frosted mugs. To this she added a green plastic plate of double-stuffed Oreos, six of them. Duncan and Tina wasted no time filling their faces.

"Just three cookies each," Mrs. Sheets said holding up her right forefinger. "And keep the glasses on the place mats. This is *such* a nice table." Her sarcastic smile *broke the ice*, as they say. The children burst into open-mouthed giggles that exposed a disgusting display of greenish brown and white cookie mash.

Ten minutes later, when the last cookie remains had been flushed with Kool Aid, Tina fixed her gaze on Duncan and waited until Mrs. Sheets had left. "So, why did you buy this crummy old house?" she asked. "My dad says no one lived in it for over fifteen years. He says it's ready to collapse."

"Yeah, I know. My dad's an odd duck. Really into history. He will be a new history professor this fall at Crowder College. Dad wanted to buy a historical house when we moved here. A *fixer-upper*, he calls it. So here we are. The furnace doesn't work. Neither does the air conditioner – not good in summertime. All the floors creak. There's one step missing at the bottom of the staircase. The ceiling in my bedroom is falling down. Only one toilet flushes, the only one that's not one hundred percent nasty. Oh, and there's a basement that has lots of rooms. My dad calls it *labyrinthine*, but I totally don't know what that means."

"*Labyrinthine* means twisty, turny, and confusing."

"Well, aren't you the smart one?"

"Actually, I am," Tina said with a snap of her head. "I have a super high IQ. My mom is a computer software engineer. She works from home. My dad is a chemical engineer, and he's the boss of research and development at the toothpaste company in Joplin. They are super smart. My big sister and I are true geniuses. And… of course I'm in the gifted program at school. Are you?"

"Probably not. My dad says I have two speeds, *slow* and *dead stop*. I like to think about things. For a long time. Sometimes don't get my work done."

"Well you need to step it up if you're my friend because I'm on – the – move. Get it?"

Duncan studied her again, remembering his mother's look. *My, my, what have we here?*"

Not waiting for a response, Tina jumped up from her chair, bussed her glass and cookie plate to the sink, and said, "I want to see the basement."

"Can't."

"Why not?"

"The stairs are too rickety so my dad boarded up the basement. He won't let me go down there until he's fixed the stairs, and that's not *high on the old priority list*, he says."

"Is there another way?"

"Well, outside there's a sloping door that covers some stairs down to the basement but it's padlocked shut. The padlock is old and rusty. It's still strong though. We don't have the key."

"Have your dad saw the lock off."

"Not happening. He doesn't want me down there and, as I said, this is not high on his priority list."

"But aren't you curious? Don't you wonder what's down there?"

"I do. I'm like my dad because I like history. It's fun to think about the olden days. Speaking of the olden days, this house is over one hundred fifty years old."

Tina's eyebrows shot up. "Really?"

"Yup. Dad did the research. No surprise there. A lady named Jenny Jamison owned it first."

"So?"

"I guess she was an old maid. Her father had this house built and my dad says it was the biggest, fanciest house in all of southwest Missouri. When her parents died, Jenny stayed on in the house. We don't know what happened to Jenny but somehow the house and everything inside came to a New York guy named Moriarty. He didn't live here most of the time and the house fell apart. Then another guy bought it. I forget his name. He worked on the place some – not a lot – but then he died. His son inherited it but he never lived here either, so the whole place just went to pot. When my dad bought it, we got the house, all the old furniture, dishes, even some old moth-eaten clothes."

"Did you say that Jenny Jamison left all her stuff here?"

"I guess so."

"Could be cool stuff in the basement. Old, old stuff."

"Could be."

Tina crossed her arms and moved her mouth from side to side, twitchy-like. "We have to go down there," she said. "We just have to."

TWO

Room Number Eight

Without a further word, Tina ran home. She just up and ran home. Duncan didn't see her again until the next day when he wandered out to the back porch carrying a green plastic plate with a circular slice of watermelon. Mrs. Sheets had told him he could slobber and spit on the porch. (Her exact words were, *I don't want that juice and those little black seeds in the house. Out you go.* She meant *slobber* and *spit*.) Duncan had to admit that his mom was a wee bit odd herself. Not as odd as his dad, but still a touch off. As he sat down on the porch, his feet dangling over the edge, he heard a buzzing sound around the corner. Curious, he hefted himself off the edge of the porch and plodded toward the sound.

There, to his disbelief, he beheld Tina Ng standing on the outside doors to the basement, extracting screws from the hinges with a power drill set on reverse.

"Tina, what are you doing?" Duncan shouted, pitching his slice of watermelon aside and racing at his top speed (slow) toward the basement door. "Stop! What are you doing?"

"It should be quite clear what I'm doing," she said. "I'm checking out your basement."

"No you aren't. You don't have permission. My dad will flip his lid if he finds out what you're doing. Stop now!"

"Chill. I won't take anything. Won't break anything. I want to see what's in a one-hundred-fifty year old basement. You come with me."

"No. I'll get into a heap of trouble. I might even get a licking. I haven't had a licking in two years but I remember it. When my dad spanks, it hurts. My mom doesn't hurt but my dad sure does. So screw those screws back in."

"Come on, Duncan. Here's the plan. We'll get these screws out, just on one side. We'll slip downstairs and pull the door back over the opening. I've got a flashlight, and it's not just any flashlight. It's a super wonderful three-thousand lumen high intensity LED flashlight. It'll be like daylight down there."

"Nothing doing."

"You afraid?"

"Yes."

Tina cackled. "Of the boogie man?"

"No, my folks."

"Come on. Thirty minutes, no more."

"Not going down there."

"Fifteen?"

Duncan hesitated.

"I saw that," Tina said, pointing her skinny finger at Duncan's head. "You looked around. You looked to see if anyone is watching. You want to see the basement. Admit it."

"Do not."

"Do too. Come on. Just fifteen minutes."

Duncan scanned the horizon again, longer this time. Nothing moved in the quiet countryside except the flutter of oak leaves in high breezes. Duncan knew by now Mrs. Sheets would be scrubbing the one hundred percent nasty toilets. Professor Sheets had gone to Crowder to move an impressive library of history books into his new office. Quiet enough. Safe enough.

Duncan shrugged. "Okay. But just fifteen minutes."

Tina zipped out the last screw and the two children slid the door from the hinge side, just wide enough for Duncan to wedge through the opening. (Tina could have slipped through much earlier.) They pulled the door over the opening and Tina ignited the flashlight. They eased forward pawing aside years of accumulated cobwebs filled with insects sucked dry by their eight-legged captors. The bright beam of the flashlight sent two large spiders skittering along ruined webs to the safety of a crack in the wall.

Tina and Duncan shuddered each time a strand of spider silk slid across a cheek or arm. Still swiping at the clingy silk, they crossed into a large room. Tina panned the basement with the flashlight beam exposing thick oak floor joists a few feet above their heads. "Look...," Her pointer finger entered the flashlight beam. "Ten doors. All shut. How totally cool. Let's check them out."

"Hold on," Duncan said, closing his hand around her arm.

She jerked her arm away. "Keep your hands to yourself! I'm Asian. Asian girls are small. My arms are skinny, but I can smack you senseless. I know karate moves. Get it?"

Duncan stepped back, his hands raised high. "Okay... okay. Sorry. No offense. But let's not go wild here. I think we should pick one room and concentrate on it. Then we should leave."

"With nine doors unopened? How dumb is that?"

"We only have fifteen minutes."

"That's plenty of time to check everything out."

Without waiting for further debate, Tina ran to the first door on the left and opened it. Training her flashlight on the interior of the room, she spotted nothing but old wooden crates with bolts, nuts, hooks, nails, and chains, all rusted and useless. Several careful glances confirmed that there was nothing of much interest in room number one.

In one quick move, Tina proceeded to the second door. Two discarded toilets and a dozen old crockery jugs filled with nothing but dead bugs ringed the room.

"Those toilets are better than the ones upstairs," Duncan said, his voice tinged with disappointment.

"You should tell your mom," Tina said.

"Nothing doing."

"Okay, on to number three."

The third room contained two clothes racks made of old pipes. Hanging from them were dozens of dresses and petticoats, shredded, moth-eaten, and mildewed with age. Tina reached up to touch one of the once-elegant dresses and it crumbled to the floor in a pile of threads.

"That's not good," Duncan said.

"Look, I didn't mean to ruin that dress. It was falling apart anyway. How was I to know that it would turn into fluff just by touching it? Seriously? Were you planning to save it?"

"No, I guess not. Let's move on."

They found nothing exciting in rooms four, five, and six. A big fat nothing. However, spirits were lifted slightly in room seven. It housed several old oaken file cabinets that held promise. Something for a later day.

Suddenly, they heard steps on the floor above.

"Shhh," Duncan said, grasping Tina's arm once again. "My mom is down from the upstairs bathrooms. We better be going."

Tina jerked her arm away. "One more room. Number eight is the one. Let's go... *bonanza* time."

"Please, Tina. We have to get out of here."

"Just a few seconds. Come on."

Tina grasped the round glass knob on the door to room number eight, turned it, and pulled the door open. It gave off an earsplitting, low-pitched groan. She stopped pulling on the knob. Both children sucked in a deep breath and held it. Even in the back glow of the flashlight, Tina could see that Duncan's round face had turned so red he looked like a freshly picked garden beet. They waited in silence for at least thirty seconds until they could hold their breath no longer. They gulped fresh air and held their breath again. Nothing. The footsteps had stopped upstairs.

After what seemed an eternity, the footsteps started again and, to the children's relief, they became fainter and fainter. Mrs. Sheets was heading back upstairs. Duncan put a finger under Tina's nose.

"That was close. Too close. This is it. The last room. Then we leave."

"Okay. Okay."

They slid through the door, Tina first, and swept their eyes over the contents of room number eight. Unlike the other rooms with concrete floors, this one had a dirt floor. There were shelves all around with some old glass jars and rusty cans arranged in haphazard fashion. In the center of the room stood a simple wooden table, encrusted with mold and decades of dust.

"Look at this dirt floor," Duncan said. "It's as smooth as concrete."

"And flat," Tina said. "No bumps at all, except..." Tina crisscrossed the beam of her flashlight on a small rise in the dirt floor in the far dark corner of the room. "See that bump, Duncan?"

"Where?"

Tina wiggled her flashlight. "There. In the light beam. See?"

Duncan squinted. "Yeah, maybe."

"I want to check it out."

"We don't have time."

"We're making time. Now get with it."

The two children knelt by the rise in the earthen floor and scratched away the dirt with jar lids. After several minutes, a wooden handle emerged. They dug faster until their efforts revealed a box about two feet long, one foot wide, and ten inches deep.

"Oh boy," Tina said. "Jackpot!"

Duncan's eyes widened. "What do you suppose is in the box?"

"I don't know. Let's pull it out."

When they had freed the box, they placed it on the table.

"It's locked," Tina said.

"Don't have time now. We have to get out of here. We need to take it somewhere and hide it. Got any ideas?"

"Of course I have ideas. I'm a genius, remember? There's an old barn in back of our place. I go out there all the time. My mom and dad never check up on me when I'm in the barn. It still has hay in the loft. Let's hide the box in the hay."

Duncan nodded. It seemed a reasonable plan to him. "Now we *have* to go!"

"Fine. Pick up the box. Remember...my arms are too skinny."

She was rather funny, Duncan had to admit, even if she had no respect for other people's private property – or their feelings, for that matter. "Okay. I'll get it but let's keep in mind that this box belongs to the Sheets family. So don't get any ideas about what you will do with whatever we find inside."

"Of course," she said with a thin smile.

Much more quickly than one might have predicted, Duncan and Tina raced out of the basement, replaced the door, and screwed the hinges back in place. Without warning, Tina snatched the box from

Duncan's grip and raced down the lane to her house, weaving from side-to-side under the weight of the drill and flashlight under one arm and the newfound box in the other. Duncan watched her go for several long seconds before retrieving his watermelon slice and flicking off the ants. He took a bite and a deep breath. What was it with this girl, the first and only friend he had in his new town? He supposed time would tell, but in the meantime he felt a weird combination of excitement and dread.

Was room number eight really the jackpot?

THREE

The Box

The next morning, after he had finished his chores, Duncan shot through the dilapidated front screen door of his house and ran at top speed (slow) down the lane to Tina's place. As he drew near to the Ng residence, he noticed that the ranch-style house rested in a perfectly landscaped yard complete with several fountains, flower-lined rock pathways, and five sculpted trees. He'd seen trees like these at *Phatt Wok*, the fancy Chinese restaurant in Miami, whence he and his family had just moved.

The only thing that marred this perfect scene was the old barn perched on a slight rise forty yards behind the house. It projected into the sky in craggy dignity. Its gray boards, weathered over many years, told of an earlier time of horses, buggies, pitchforks, and plows. Boards were missing here and there but Duncan could tell the old thing was erect and sturdy, no lean to it. The missing boards provided a glimpse of the interior but little could be seen in the dark recesses. It seemed a shadowy and safe place to store the *box of treasures.*

Since finding the box, Duncan dreamed about what it might contain. He was certain it hid amazing treasures, maybe even old gold coins and hand-drawn maps that would lead to even more riches. He couldn't wait to open it. Seeing no doorbell, he knocked on the polished wooden door.

A few seconds later, the door opened and a tiny lady, not much taller than Duncan, opened the door and peered out.

"Herro," she said. "You must be Mister Sheets." Her voice sounded like a tinkling wind chime.

"Her-... I mean, hello," Duncan said, annoyed with himself. Every time someone spoke to him in a foreign accent (which wasn't all that often), he would slip into the accent himself. He couldn't seem to help it. One time he nearly got into a fight with four Hispanic boys at school when he mimicked their accent. If Mrs. Hunsacker, the sixth-grade teacher, hadn't happened by at just the right time, they might have pounded him.

"Prease to come in," Mrs. Ng said, her eyes narrowing to tiny slits as she smiled. "I Tina mother – Ming Ng. I get Tina."

Ming Ng? Seriously?

As Mrs. Ng scuttled away, Duncan stood in the hallway and marveled at the perfect arrangement of furniture and accessories. And so clean. Not a mote of dust could be seen anywhere. The wooden furniture gleamed with polish. Before him, in the living room, bright red walls surrounded two long white couches accented with red and white pillows. On a low black coffee table between the couches rested a porcelain statue of a fluffy white dog that looked Chinese. Duncan couldn't rightly say why it looked like a Chinese dog. It just did. Seven paper lanterns hung from the ceiling – four red and three white with dangling tassels. The room appeared so elegant to Duncan that he was afraid to walk into it.

He noticed near the door four sets of shoes arrayed in perfect order, laid out in Goldilocks fashion. Papa's to the left, then mama's, then Tina's sister's, which were strange silver studded black platform shoes, and finally Tina's. He took off his own sneakers, pushing down on the heel with the toe of his other foot, something against which his mother had repeatedly warned him. "You'll ruin those shoes that way," she would say. On this occasion, he ignored his mother's warning.

As he placed his shoes next to Tina's, she strode out of the hallway into the room and gave a quick glance in Duncan's direction. Without a word, she marched into the kitchen, her mother and Duncan in tow.

"Would you prease to have some hot tea?" Mrs. Ng asked, again with a wide smile. Her eyes narrowed to crescent lines.

Duncan looked at Tina who stood next to her mother, her arms crossed over her chest and wrapped around her body. She had no expression.

Hot tea on a hot August day? That made no sense to Duncan.

As if reading his mind, Mrs. Ng said, "It strange, but hot drink make you coo' down. Hot drink trick brain, make brain think it hotter than it is. Brain tell coo-ring system in body to go to work. Bingo... you coo' down. You see?"

Duncan shrugged his shoulders, having never heard such a thing. "Okay, if you say so."

"Good," Mrs. Ng said. "Prease to sit at table. I will brew tea. You rike some gummy candy?"

"Sure," Duncan said.

"You ever make gummy candy?"

"No, ma'am."

"I show you while tea brewing. Tina, prease to get three gumi tsureta."

Tina opened a cupboard and withdrew three colorful foil packages. They had many Chinese characters on them with images of happy little children, kittens, and pandas. Mrs. Ng opened one package and withdrew a plastic tray along with three smaller foil pouches and a straw. She cut off one corner of the tray that had been formed to make a small cup. From a pitcher she poured four little cups of water into the tray. Then she stirred in some yellowish powder from one of the pouches until it made a gel in the tray. She bent the straw and lowered the shorter end into the tray. Over the bent end, she poured couple of teaspoons of powder from another package. Slowly she withdrew the straw. As she did so, she pulled out a solid strip of gooey material.

"Whoa! That's cool," Duncan said, his eyes widening at the little miracle.

"It fun to make," Mrs. Ng said. "You try."

Tina ripped open her package and had her piece of candy made before Duncan could even fill his tray with water. She waited for him to finish, drumming her fingers on the table. "Let's try them," she said, once Duncan had drawn his gooey strip out of the gelatin.

Both children bit off a chunk of the candy. Chewy, Duncan

thought but delicious. "Kind of like fruit roll-ups," he said.

They had enough powder to make several more strips to go with their tea. When they finished this fascinating snack, Tina announced to her mother they were going out to the barn.

"Prease to be careful," Mrs. Ng said. "Watch for snake."

"Snakes?" Duncan said, suddenly alarmed.

"Yes, we've seen copperheads in the barn. If you don't bother them, they won't bother you."

Leaving Duncan in nervous agitation, Tina ran to her room and returned with several kid magazines to cover the real purpose of their going to the barn. "We're going to read in the hay," she told her mother as they burst through the back door in a full run to the old gray barn. Tina arrived a full five seconds before Duncan.

"Where are the snakes?" Duncan asked, as they stepped into the barn.

"Sometimes they're in the hay."

"Where's the box?"

"In the hay."

"Oh great!"

"Quit worrying about the snakes," Tina said looking at Duncan with annoyance. "You can be *such* a wuss."

Quick as a jackrabbit, Tina scampered up a shaky ladder to the loft and disappeared. A few seconds later, her head reappeared over the edge of the loft. "You come up the ladder and get the box. It's too heavy. I nearly dropped it getting it up here."

"I'm not climbing up that old ladder. It might break."

"It will not break. Get with it!"

Very gingerly, Duncan put his right foot on the first rung of the ladder. He tested it with three tentative bounces and, when it didn't break, he ventured another step, then another, until he was high enough to grab the box. When they had it on the floor, they sat cross-legged and pondered their next move.

"How will we open the padlock?" Duncan asked.

"Can you pick locks?"

"No, of course not. Why would I know how to pick a lock?"

"Well, it would be helpful," Tina said. "We must break the lock off. See that old sledgehammer in the corner? Go get it. I'll find a rock to put under the lock."

It took Duncan four shots on the lock with the sledgehammer

before it broke apart. Just as they were getting ready to open the lock, a strain of music floated into the barn.

"What's that?" Duncan asked.

"Must be something going on at the George Washington Carver National Monument. Maybe a music festival or something."

"Oh yeah, I remember now. My dad said we would be living almost next door to the Monument. Said we'd go visit it sometime soon. Have you been there, Tina?"

"Hundreds of times."

"Hundreds? Really?"

"Not hundreds, silly. When you say *hundreds*, it doesn't mean multiples of ten times ten. It just means *a lot* or *a bunch*. Sheesh! Don't you know anything?"

"Okay so then how many times have you actually gone?"

Tina pursed her lips to the side as she thought for a moment. "Maybe ten."

"Is it cool?"

"Pretty cool the first couple of times but then it gets boring. You will go to the Monument on a school field trip. I guarantee it."

"Ugh! Don't remind me. School begins in three days."

"Yes, next Monday. Now quit jabbering. Let's see what's in the box."

Gingerly they lifted the lid of the box and with their heads touching, Duncan and Tina peered into the red velvet interior. The lid itself contained a pocket secured by a small locked hasp. In the bottom of the box, on the left, tied in a faded purple ribbon were dozens of letters. The top one was addressed to *My dearest Jenny.*

"Jenny," Duncan said. "That must be Jenny Jamison."

"Well duh! Letters addressed to Jenny Jamison found in a box in Jenny Jamison's house would be no big surprise."

"I wonder who they're from."

"Probably just old love letters. *Bor*-ing."

They continued to examine the contents of the box. A black leather wallet lay next to the letters. Carefully, Duncan picked up the wallet and opened it. "Holy cow," he said. "There's a ton of money."

Tina snatched the wallet from Duncan's hand. "I'll count it. I can count faster than you." She riffled through the bills, her lips moving in silent calculation. When she finished, she looked up at

Duncan, her eyes wide. "Dunc, there are fifteen old $500 bills and 25 $100 bills. That's $10,000!"

"Whoa!"

"Whoa is right! What are we going to do?"

"Nothing right now," Duncan said, retrieving the wallet from Tina and laying it back in its red velvet nest. "Let's see what else we have."

A wooden box, one-foot square, lay to the right of the wallet. Duncan pulled it out, undid the small metal clasp and opened the box. He withdrew an old pocketknife with a white bone handle and two blades. "Hmm," he murmured. He returned the pocketknife to its place and picked up three rocks. "This black one is obsidian," he said. "And I think this gray one is pumice, but I don't know about the red one. Do you?"

"No," Tina said.

"Really, so there *is* something the great genius doesn't know."

Tina stuck her tongue out. Duncan smiled.

Tina reached into the wooden box and pulled out two black and white photographs. The first one pictured two men, one African American, and one white standing on a porch. Both wore old-timey suits with those scratchy starched white collars that men once wore.

"Who do you suppose those guys are?" Duncan asked.

"Well, the black guy looks like George Washington Carver," Tina said. "I don't know the other guy."

"And who's the lady standing with George Washington Carver in this other picture."

"Might be Jenny Jamison."

"Good guess. Wait, let me see that." Duncan brought the picture closer to his eyes. "That's the porch on my house."

"Sure is," Tina said. "Gotta be Jenny Jamison."

"That's pretty cool. George Washington Carver was at my house. Boy would my dad freak out over that."

"Well, you're not telling him."

"I don't know. We have to report the $10,000."

Tina shot up from her sitting position and pushed Duncan onto the hay-strewn floor. She sat on his chest and pinned his arms. "Get this straight Duncan Sheets. You aren't telling anyone about what's in this box. Get it!"

Her efforts to pin Duncan were too puny. He sat up and she toppled backward. "We won't decide right now," he said pushing her aside, "but we have to do the right thing. Let's see what else is in the box."

Tina felt around in the smaller wooden box until her fingers touched a tiny skeleton key, an inch long, which had been wedged into the corner.

"This must be for the lid," Tina said.

Sure enough, when she inserted the key into the lock and gave it a turn to the right, the pocket fell open to reveal several papers. They contained what appeared to be scientific recipes and formulae.

"What do you make of these?" Duncan asked.

Tina studied them for the better part of two minutes. "These are chemistry notes about oil, I think. I'm not sure what they mean."

"Look here," Duncan said. "A letter to Doctor George Washington Carver, care of Tuskegee Institute, Tuskegee, Alabama. It's written on old brown paper in an old brown paper envelope."

Tina rubbed the envelope between her thumb and forefinger. "Look at all these weird postmarks and stamps. Can you read them?"

"They seem kind of rubbed out," Duncan said. "I think the first postmark is *Bruxelles.*"

"Gotta be Brussels," Tina said.

"Yeah and look here. There's another postmark from *Saint Nazaire*. Where is that?"

"France, maybe?" Tina said. "Could be the letter went from Brussels to Saint Nazaire and then across the ocean to New York because here is another postmark from New York."

"What do you make of this last stamp, *SS Mont Blanc?*"

"Might be the ship this letter came across the Atlantic on," Tina said.

"Good guess. Must not have had airplanes in those days."

"Of course they had airplanes!" Tina said, looking at Duncan as if he were some kind of mindless slug. "They just couldn't yet fly across the ocean. Now let's have a look a the letter. Get with it!"

Slowly, Duncan lifted the flap of the envelope and extracted the letter. He and Tina peered at strange words written in cursive.

"I have no idea what this says," Duncan said, turning his gaze on Tina. "It looks like it's in German."

"Me neither. Can you make out the name at the bottom?"

"Looks like *Rudolf Diesel*."

Both children shrugged.

"What about these?" Tina shoved two newspaper articles under his nose. "Can you read this writing?"

"No. These old newspaper articles look like they're in German too," he said.

Tina tried to sound out the words. "The headline on this one says, *Inventer Verschwindet in der Nordsee*. What does that mean Duncan?"

"I don't know. I don't speak German but my dad does. Sheets is the English spelling of a German name which I can't pronounce. My dad and grandfather talk in German all the time. He'll know what it means."

"Nothing doing. You're not taking this to your dad."

Duncan stared at Tina for a long moment, studying her. "We'll see," he said, his voice low, authoritative. "We won't decide right now."

At that very moment, they heard Mrs. Ng calling. "Tina... Tina... time to go to Neosho."

Tina rolled her eyes and sighed. "I have to go. Mom has a doctor's appointment in Neosho."

"Well then, let's hide the box. We can come back tomorrow."

"I can't. Tomorrow we are going to Kansas City to visit my aunt and uncle for the weekend." She stuck a forefinger under Duncan's nose. "And you don't go looking at this while I'm gone. We're a team. Get it?"

"I don't think I can anyway," Duncan said. "We're going to Silver Dollar City tomorrow as the last fling before school starts. Then on Sunday, we will try a new church. I think it's Presbyterian."

"I don't know what a Presbyterian is. We don't go to church."

"Why not?"

"We're geniuses and know that there isn't a God."

"You sure about that, Tina?"

"Yes, my dad said so."

Duncan let it go.

"Tina… Tina… Time to go."

"I gotta go. You close it up and take it up in the loft. Hide it under the hay."

With that, Tina shot out of the barn leaving Duncan with a treasure trove far more valuable than he'd ever imagined.

FOUR

Gone

That Sunday evening, Mrs. Sheets put a hand on her son's shoulder. "When you finish loading those dishes in the dishwasher, go upstairs and get your school supplies rounded up and lay out your school clothes. We are up early in the morning. And be careful around that missing step."

Duncan's head flopped with a groan. "*Schoooool. Ugh.*"

He had finished placing the last three plates in the dishwasher when he heard a knock on the door. As soon as he opened it, Tina grabbed the front of his shirt in her tight little fist and jerked him onto the porch. "It's gone! Gone! Gone! Gone!" she said, her voice a strained hiss.

"Slow down, Tina. What's gone?"

"The box."

"What? The *box*? How?"

Tina paced back and forth on the porch. "My dad! My crazy dad had the barn torn down while we were in Kansas City. He didn't tell me he was going to do it. Some Amish guys came here Saturday, tore down the barn, and hauled off all the lumber. They spread the hay all over and there's no box! I've looked everywhere for it. Those Amish guys took it. It's gone. Ten thousand bucks!

What do we do?"

Duncan tried to stay calm in the face of this terrible news. His cherry red complexion had faded to a light pink, which made his crop of carrot-colored hair even more carroty. "Okay. We have to remain calm, Tina. Let's sit down and figure out what to do."

"What's to think about? It's gone. Those Amish guys got the money."

"Sit, Tina. Please."

She glared at Duncan for several long seconds before plopping down on one of the green metal chairs. She stared into the late summer sky.

After a moment of silence, Duncan said, "We have to tell my dad."

Tina bounced out of her chair and thrust her forefinger toward Duncan's face. "Nothing doing. He will get me in trouble with my dad."

"Maybe not. I'll tell him it was my idea to go into the basement."

"Why would you do that?"

Duncan shrugged. "My dad will get mad but he will be fair. We did something wrong and we need to fess up. I'll get punished, but it's better to get it off my chest and take what's coming."

Tina crossed her arms and scowled. She gave a big heave-ho breath. "Okay. Let's get it over with."

They trudged up the stairs and into Professor Sheet's home office. He sat in a big blue overstuffed chair reading a book under the low light of a brass floor lamp. It didn't take Tina long to note the family resemblance. Both he and Duncan had carrot tops, ruby-red cheeks, and round bellies. She marveled at Professor Sheets' handlebar mustache that curled into a full loop on each end. He greeted them with a white-toothed smile under his loopy-de-loop mustache.

"So this must be your new friend, Tina," he said laying aside his book. "To what do I owe this pleasant visit?"

"We have something to tell you, dad," Duncan said. His voice sounded as if he had just choked on a gumdrop.

"Sounds serious," Professor Sheets said.

"Yeah, it kinda is."

With that Duncan explained in a hushed voice the unearthing, hiding, and opening of the box. He described in careful detail each item in the box as if to prolong his report. Maybe, he thought, if he took a long time describing the contents of the box, he would stave off any possible punishment. True to his word, he never once mentioned Tina's part in the whole caper. When Duncan finished, he looked up at his father, but not into his eyes. Too scary. Instead, he fixed his gaze on his father's chin. Professor Sheets studied the two children while flicking the right loop of his mustache back and forth with his forefinger.

For some reason, Duncan counted the flicks. Twenty-one. Twenty-one flicks in dead silence can be a pretty disturbing experience.

"I see," Professor Sheets said as he heaved himself out of his chair. Duncan and Tina stepped back, eyes wide. "I would like you to go out on the porch while I talk this over with Duncan's mother."

Tina and Duncan sat on two green metal porch chairs and waited. The shrill humming of a thousand cicadas did nothing to calm their nerves.

"What do you suppose will happen?" Tina asked.

Duncan shrugged. "Dunno."

They waited.

"How was Silver Dollar City?" Tina asked, trying to break the long tense silence.

"Didn't go. Dad had to do stuff in his office. We didn't have time. Went to the George Washington Carver National Monument instead."

"How was that?"

"Pretty cool, actually. I learned a lot, mostly from this old guy named Gideon."

"Who's Gideon?"

"Gideon is a retired minister but knows a lot about George Washington Carver. When he retired, he signed up at the Monument as a volunteer. He said if we wanted to come back some time, he would give us a private tour and tell us some cool stuff about George Washington Carver. You up for that?"

"Maybe."

"Course I'll probably be grounded for five years."

Just then, Professor Sheets and his wife appeared. Professor

Sheets leaned back against the porch rail. Mrs. Sheets stood to the side, her arms crossed. Not a good sign.

"Well Mister Duncan and Miss Tina…" Professor Sheets said. Using *Mister* and *Miss* was not a good sign either. "Our next step is to pay a visit to Miss Tina's parents."

Tina sucked in a deep breath. Before she could say anything, Professor Sheets went on, not taking his eyes off Tina. "I think your parents should be told. Come now, it's a nice evening for a walk down the lane."

Upon arriving at the Ng residence, Tina opened the polished wooden front door and reluctantly invited the Sheets into her house. She called for her mother and father. Duncan pointed to the shoes lined up beside the door and the Sheets removed theirs, aligning them in a neat array. Mr. Ng, dressed in a white polo shirt, white tennis shorts, and white athletic socks, strode into the room. Mrs. Ng slipped behind him.

"Marty Ng," he said in a jaunty voice while extending his hand. Unlike his daughter, he pronounced their last name *Ing*, which was not a sound, Duncan noted, but a syllable and much easier to say. There could be no doubt that Marty Ng was of Asian descent but, unlike his wife, he had no trace of an accent.

With the introductions completed and all seated on the white furniture, Professor Sheets asked Duncan to repeat his admission, omitting nothing. To focus his thoughts, Duncan stared at the white porcelain Chinese dog the whole time he pled his guilt. The dog stared back.

"Tina…," Mr. Ng said as soon as Duncan had finished. "Just what was your role in all of this?" Tina stared at her swinging legs. "Look at me, Tina. I want to know just what part you played. You borrowed my drill. I wondered why at the time. Can you explain this?"

"It's more my fault than Duncan's," she blurted. "It was all my idea." With that Tina crossed her arms over her chest, slumped over in her chair, and burst into tears.

After several awkward seconds filled with sobs, Professor Sheets said in a calm voice, "Well, at least both of you told us the truth. We must decide the appropriate consequence but for now, we need to find the box. It contains not only money but valuable historical items."

"Do you think we should call the police?" Marty Ng asked.

"We could but I know the Amish to be a moral, peace-loving people. I hate to call the police down on them. If we had the contact information, I'd just as soon get in touch with them and see if they can help us find the box. That is, if they took it in the first place."

"You're right," Marty Ng said. "I suppose it's possible that someone else could have come, found the box in the hay, and made off with it."

"I'm free next Saturday," Professor Sheets said. "If necessary, the kids and I could pay the Amish leaders a visit."

"Oh, Delbert," Mrs. Sheets said. "Do you think you should involve the children further?"

Delbert? Really? Despite the seriousness of the situation, it was all Tina could do to keep from laughing through her sniffles.

"Actually, I think it would be a good experience for them," Delbert Sheets said. "They could see how other folks live."

"It's okay with me," Marty Ng said. "Tina will go with you."

"Dad, I don't…"

"No argument young lady," Mr. Ng said holding up his hand. "You are a part of this problem and you shall be part of the solution." He turned to Professor Sheets. "So, about the barn… I worked with a guy named Hudspeth, Dokie Hudspeth. He's a contractor who manages Amish crews. The Amish don't drive, you know. So Dokie Hudspeth brought them over in a van and another non-Amish guy drove a flatbed truck to haul off the lumber. Hudspeth and the Amish folk are located a couple of hours away from here in a little town called Seymour. Better call Hudspeth first, before driving to Seymour."

"Good idea," Professor Sheets said. "I'll do that."

With Hudspeth's phone number in hand, Professor Sheets thanked the Ngs and ushered his wife and son out the door. They did not see Tina's sister staring at them from her bedroom window. In the shadows, she twirled her blue hair and flicked a tongue over the little silver ball that pierced her lower lip.

Once back at their run-down old house, Professor Sheets called Dokie Hudspeth. "I see…," "Uh -huh…," "Uh-huh…," "Uh-huh…," and "How do I find this Isaac Beiler?" were the only snatches of conversation Duncan could hear.

"What did he say, Dad?" Duncan asked when his father closed the call with a tap of his finger.

"Says he knows nothing about a box. There was a guy named Isaac Beiler who oversaw the Amish tearing down the barn. We need to talk to him."

"Did you get his number?"

"Well, that's a problem. The Amish don't carry cell phones and don't have phones in their homes. Mr. Hudspeth told me that the Beilers have a phone shanty, kind of like an old-time phone booth, about thirty yards from their house. They won't hear the phone to answer unless they happen to be walking by the shanty. Our best bet is to go to the Beiler's house. So, road trip on Saturday."

~~~

The following Saturday, Professor Sheets loaded Tina and Duncan in the back seat of his blue Ford minivan. They headed south on highway Fifty-nine to catch U.S. Sixty eastbound to Seymour.

After ten miles of silence, Professor Sheets said, "I'm curious about those letters and photographs you found. As a historian I'm thinking that could be an important collection. The connection between Rudolf Diesel and George Washington Carver is interesting, to say the least."

"Who is Rudolf Diesel?" Duncan asked.

"I'll show you," Professor Sheets said, as he jerked the steering wheel to the right and pulled into a gas station. "See that green handle on the gas pump? What does it say?"

"Diesel."

"Right you are. Rudolf Diesel invented the diesel engine."

"And George Washington Carver knew him?"

"So it would seem, but..." Professor Sheets glanced back over the seat at his son and raised a forefinger, "the interesting thing is how and why they knew each other. That's what cranks up history professors."

Duncan and Tina glanced at each other, both suppressing smiles at the image of a *cranked up history professor.* Professor Sheets *is* an odd duck, she thought to herself. Yet, somehow she sensed that his interest in history *may* have warded off the punishment they should have received for breaking into the basement. He must have become so excited at what they had found that he forgot to ground Duncan or, just maybe he decided not to punish his son. As the Sheets were leaving the Ngs earlier in the week, she glimpsed the professor winking at her dad, a dad-to-dad signal. Could this trip to Seymour be a substitute for the expected punishment? Time had to be on their side, didn't it? Wouldn't the passing of time soften the blow?

They stopped for burgers in Springfield (a veggie burger for vegetarian Tina) and pressed on to Seymour. When they arrived in the Seymour area, Professor Sheets went into Uncle Rooster's Restaurant and asked for directions to the Beiler farm.

"Head on east to Cedar Tree Road and go south, 'bout a mile or two," the waitress said. "Big gray house on the right. No electrical wires to the house or barn. Sturdy mailbox says *Beiler.* Big windmill. Can't miss the place."

Cedar Tree Road turned out to be a curvy two-lane street, potholed and bumpy. The Amish must have experienced rough rides in their black horse-drawn buggies, or so Duncan thought. In their strange olden-days clothing, farmers looked up from their fieldwork as Professor Sheets and the children drove by. Professor Sheets explained that the Amish prefer to work close to the land as a family. "The children have chores to do from an early age. When they finish the eighth grade, they take their place in the world. How would you like that?"

"Sounds great!" Duncan said.

"Not for me. I'm going to school until I'm thirty," Tina said with a sharp little nod. "I'm getting a doctorate and then a post-doctorate in biophysics."

"Well good for you," Professor Sheets said. "I like a person with ambition."

Duncan stared out the car window.

Upon arrival at the Beiler farm, a tall sturdy man in a gray shirt, black pants with suspenders, and a wide-brimmed straw hat emerged from the barn door. He stroked his long chin whiskers and waited for the visitors to step out of the car.

"Good afternoon," Professor Sheets said. "Isaac Beiler?"

"Yes, sir. What can I do for you?"

For the next several minutes, Professor Sheets explained the purpose of their visit. Isaac Beiler listened but made no comment. A period of uncomfortable silence followed.

"I know about this box," Isaac Beiler said. "My sons brought it to me. They say they found it in a field. You say it is yours and that it was in the barn we tore down?"

"Yes, sir."

"Well, the box is gone," Isaac Beiler said.

"Where is it?" Professor Sheets asked.

"I sold it to an antique dealer. I think he was from Springfield. He was here looking to buy some old crocks and butter churns. I showed him the box, and he said he'd buy that too."

"If you don't mind my asking, how much did you sell the box for?"

"A hundred dollars."

Tina could contain herself no longer. "A hundred dollars! Are you kidding me? You sold it for a hundred dollars!"

Isaac Beiler shot Tina a stern look. He did not answer her.

Professor Sheets jumped back into the conversation. "Do you know the dealer's name?"

"No. Everything was on a cash basis. No check. No business card."

"What about the wallet?" Tina asked with alarm ringing in her voice.

Professor Sheets put his hand on Tina's shoulder in an effort to quiet her down. "It is a good question," he said. "There was a black wallet. Do you remember that?"

"I did not see a wallet," Isaac Beiler said. "Just some letters and photographs. Also an old pocketknife and three rocks."

"When we last saw it," Professor Sheets said, "there was also a black leather wallet. It contained money. You didn't see that?"

"No, but I will call my sons."

Isaac Beiler marched back to the barn and hollered through the door, "Daniel, Benuel. Herkommen."

"That means *come here* in German," Professor Sheets whispered.

Two strapping teen-aged boys appeared in the doorway of the barn and followed their father back to where Professor Sheets stood. The boys wore the same clothes as their father but sported no beards.

"Eine mappe. Did you see eine mappe, a wallet, im der box?"

"No wallet," the boys said in unison.

"You must tell the truth," Isaac Beiler said.

Daniel and Benuel glanced at each other.

"It's the truth," Daniel, the older, said. "We did not see a wallet."

"And where did you find this box?" Isaac asked.

"In a field."

"What field?"

The boys looked at each other again. Both cast their eyes to the ground.

"The field where we took down the barn," Daniel said, his voice soft and uneasy. "When we found the box we hid it under some wood on the truck. When we came home, we decided we should give it to you."

"You did not tell me you found it by the barn," Isaac Beiler said, his voice low and cool. "That was wrong." The boys made no response. "Go back to work," Isaac Beiler said. "I will talk with you later." Looking Professor Sheets in the eye, he continued, "I am sorry for my sons. They are good boys. This is a mistake and I will deal with them. What do you want me to do?"

Professor Sheets took a deep breath. "I'm not sure this rises to the level of legal action. The boys made a mistake. Perhaps they did not even consider it theft. They probably thought the contents of the barn were theirs to keep. You sold the box in good faith thinking it to be discarded property. Can you describe the dealer for me?"

Isaac Beiler nodded. "He was a short, black-haired man, black eyes, mustache, no beard. He had a scar on his forehead above his right eye. Dressed in a fancy English way, polished leather shoes, tan pants, and one of them Hawaiian shirts, I think you call them. Big flowers all over the shirt."

"Thank you," Professor Sheets said. "Here is my new business card. I work at Crowder College in Neosho. If you think or hear of anything more… "

Isaac Beiler assured them that he would be in touch if anything new surfaced. With that, he turned and walked toward the barn.

FIVE

The Dream Knife

On the twisty, bumpy return trip up Cedar Tree Road, Duncan and Tina pressed Professor Sheets with questions.

"Why do they wear those old-fashioned clothes," Tina asked.

"Well," Professor Sheets said. "They want to preserve the traditional ways of their people. This is the way their ancestors dressed in Germany and the way their forefathers dressed when they came to America."

"But why?"

"They think that many of our modern developments, our technology and such, are dangerous and can draw them away from their devotion to God and family. So they avoid technology and, I suppose, as a symbol of the old ways, they wear traditional clothing."

"Is that why they don't use electricity, and tractors, and stuff?" Duncan asked.

"Yes. Exactly."

"That's dumb," Tina said.

Professor Sheets glanced over the front seat and raised his right forefinger. "Think about it this way. In our society, we all do our own thing. We don't do as many things as a family anymore. The

Amish, by using horses to plow and harvest, remain close to the land. They work together as a family. In that way they are nearer to the life lived by our Lord and the people of His time. All of our modern conveniences can be a distraction. Think about watching television, surfing the Web, texting, iPods, Facebook, Tweets, and all the rest. These things can distract us from what is important in life, God and family. Modern inventions can keep us from doing things together as a family. They can also make us think we don't need God. Maybe the Amish know something we don't."

Tina pursed her lips and twisted her mouth to the side, but said nothing.

"Why do they call us English?" Duncan asked.

"I'm not sure about that," Professor Sheets said. "Perhaps when they came in contact with outsiders here in America, all they heard was the English language. So they call everybody English who isn't Amish."

The children pondered this answer, as they turned back onto Highway Sixty, westbound toward Springfield.

"Kids," Professor Sheets said. "There is an antique store a mile ahead. I'll stop and see if they recognize the antique man by the description Isaac Beiler gave us."

The *Golden Oldies and Olden Goldies Antique and Jewelry Arcade* was little more than a ramshackle barn. Rusty farm equipment, buckets, and garden tools cluttered the gravel lot making it difficult to find a place to park. Two old wringer washing machines guarded the door. The inside was honeycombed with narrow aisles and rickety display cases filled with things that Duncan and Tina didn't even recognize. While Professor Sheets spoke with the clerks, Duncan and Tina took turns picking up a strange object and asking each other what it might be.

"That's a hand brace," Professor Sheets said several minutes later, looking over Tina's shoulder at an odd tool with a long shaft and a round wooden handle. "You drill holes with it."

"Cool," Duncan said. "I wonder if the Amish still use it."

"Good chance," Professor Sheets said. "So, come on, let's go. I got what I came for."

"Did they know the guy?" Duncan asked, once they were outside the *Golden Oldies and Olden Goldies Antique and Jewelry Arcade.*

"They've seen him around but don't know his name. They think he might have an antique store in Springfield." Professor Sheets glanced at his watch. "We still have some time. Let's hit a few antique stores in Springfield and see if we can flush him out."

"My dad's a bulldog when he sets his mind on something," Duncan whispered as they climbed into the minivan. "A real bulldog."

The afternoon wore on and the *Sheets-Ng Investigative Agency*, as they now called themselves, hit six antique stores with no luck. It was the same story in each store. The clerks had seen the guy but didn't know who he was. At the last stop, an upscale, fancy pants antique store named *Precious and Priceless*, the Agency gained another clue.

Back on the road, Professor Sheets said, "They don't know the guy's name. He's not in Springfield. He runs a big antique mall down in Blue Eye, Missouri, which is right on the Arkansas line, down by Branson."

"And Silver Dollar City?" Tina asked, her eyebrows lifting.

"Close." Professor Sheet said. "But too far for today. We have to head back home."

"How about tomorrow Dad?"

"Nope. Tomorrow is the Lord's Day. We will go to church. However," Professor Sheets said, holding up his forefinger as professors do, "Monday is Labor Day and guess what?"

"School's out!" Tina and Duncan shouted in unison.

"That's right. What about this? A morning in Silver Dollar City and an afternoon looking for the Blue Eye antique guy?"

"Yes!" Duncan said with a fist pump. Tina bounced in her seat, which only tightened her seat belt.

"Since we can't go to Silver Dollar City and Blue Eye until Monday, tomorrow after church, can we take our bikes to the Monument?" Duncan asked.

"We'll see," Professor Sheets said. "Check with your mother."

~~~

Both mothers agreed to let Duncan and Tina ride their bikes to the Monument. "You go down Elder Road, to Martin Road, then to Carver Road and back the same way. No exceptions. I want to be able to trace your route if anything should happen," Mrs. Sheets said. "Understood?"

"But, Mom…"

"I mean it Duncan. No cross country stuff."

"O-*kay.*"

"And you take the family cell phone. Call me when you arrive and when you get ready to leave. Understood?"

"Yes, Mom. *Understood.*"

Mrs. Sheets didn't see Duncan's eyes roll.

The two bicyclists arrived at the Monument surprised to note that attendance was light on this Sunday afternoon. When they entered the Visitor Center, Duncan spotted an elderly gentleman deep in discussion with several other volunteers. He looked up, recognized Duncan, his eyes sparkling like sunshine on a burbling brook. Hopping up, he beckoned Tina and Duncan over to where he stood. His broad smile crinkled the wrinkles in his face and both children recognized him to be a man in love with life.

"My old friend, Duncan," he said extending his hand. "And this must be Tina."

"Yes, sir. Gideon, this is my friend Tina. Tina, this is my friend Gideon."

"How about a little tour?" Gideon said.

"Sure," Duncan said.

"Then follow me."

They headed out the south door of the Visitor Center and ambled along Carver Trail, a footpath layered with black asphalt. A high-pressure weather system had come through earlier and it was unusually cool and comfortable for early September. The sun warmed their backs and a slight leaf-riffling breeze caressed their faces. It might have been the most perfect weather day ever.

Fifty yards down Carver Trail, Gideon stopped in front of the foundation to a small cabin, just three logs high off the ground. "This is the site where George Washington Carver was born. He lived in this cabin until he was about twelve with his brother Jim," Gideon said. "It's only fourteen feet on the short side and eighteen feet on the long side. Over there on the far wall they built a rock fireplace. Only one window opened to the outside. Can you imagine how cold it must have been in the winter and how hot in the summer?"

"Wow," was all Duncan could say. Tina remained silent.

"Let's walk behind the cabin," Gideon said.

Behind the cabin, they entered thick woods and underbrush. Gideon tromped down some of the brush, making it easier for his two visitors. "We must look for ticks when we get back to the Visitor Center," he said.

"Ticks? Ticks!" Tina said. "I don't want ticks! I'm not going any further."

"We'll be but a minute," Gideon said. "Come on, I want to show you something."

Tina crossed her arms, almost all the way around her, and scowled. After more gentle coaxing, she lowered her head and tiptoed through the underbrush. Shortly, they came into a clearing filled with beautiful flowers and shrubs. A rustic sign read, *Garden of Floral Beauties.*

"I planted all of these flowers like Doctor Carver did when he was a boy," Gideon said. "He had a secret garden and called his plants his *floral beauties.*"

"It's a pretty garden," Duncan said.

The scowl had left Tina's face. She knelt to smell a light purple flower.

"What does it smell like?" Gideon asked.

"I think it smells like honey," Tina said.

"Good description," Gideon said. "This is a purple coneflower."

"Let me smell," Duncan said stooping and joining his nose with Tina's.

"I don't show everybody this garden," Gideon said. "Just like Doctor Carver, I keep it a secret and let only my special guests see it."

"This is a soft place," Duncan said. "It feels good here."

"A *soft* place. I think Doctor Carver would agree. He was a very spiritual man. Do you know what I mean by the word *spiritual*?"

"You mean like *religious*?" Tina said.

"Yes, something like that. We all have a body and a mind. Those two are easy to understand. But we also have a spirit. That's the inner part of us that gives us life. It contains the real meaning of who we are. Does that make sense?"

"Sort of," Duncan said.

"Well, keep thinking about it. It is hard to understand. It is a mystery. God talks to us in our spirit. Doctor Carver was in touch with his spirit side and that's why we can say he was a spiritual man. He believed we can get closer to our spirit if we understand and appreciate the beautiful things in nature. He spent a lifetime studying nature. It drew him closer to God. When he studied natural things, he felt closer to God, the Creator."

Tina pursed her lips and twisted them to the side. Again, she said nothing.

"Let me tell you a story about George Washington Carver," Gideon said. "He believed that God spoke to his spirit in dreams. One day, he was carving a stick with one of Moses Carver's knives (Moses was his owner) and wished he had a pocketknife of his own. One night later, he dreamed that he saw a small knife by a rind of watermelon. The rind and knife were at the foot of several corn stalks. The next morning, he raced out into Moses Carver's cornfield and there he saw the rind and knife, just where he dreamed them to be. To his dying day, he knew that God had directed him to that knife in his dream."

When Gideon looked up at Duncan and Tina, he saw that both of their jaws had dropped.

"What did the knife look like?" Duncan asked, his voice a raspy whisper.

"We don't know. In those days, they had folding knives, what we would call jackknives, and the handles were often made with bone."

"White bone?"

"Could be."

Duncan turned slowly toward Tina. Tina turned slowly toward Duncan. Could it be? The knife in the box?

"Is something wrong?" Gideon asked.

"No, nothing," Duncan and Tina said in unison.

Just then, Gideon's walkie-talkie crackled with the words, "Gideon Gifford, where are you?"

Gideon unsnapped his walkie-talkie from his belt. "By the foundation."

"Church group just arrived unscheduled. Can you lead a tour?" came the walkie-talkie voice.

"Copy that," Gideon said. He turned to his visitors. "They always ask me to do the church tours. I suppose because I'm a retired minister. Sorry, kids, I better go do this. But, I want you to come back another time. I have more stories to tell you."

"Before you go," Duncan said, "do you know who Jenny Jamison was?"

"The name *Jamison* is common in southwestern Missouri but I don't know of a Jenny Jamison. Why do you ask?"

Duncan shrugged his shoulders. "Just wondering."

"Well, I better be off," Gideon said. "I hope you can come back soon."

When Gideon was out of earshot, Tina poked Duncan in the chest. "Why did you ask about Jenny Jamison?"

"I was just curious," Duncan said. "Why are you so huffy?"

"The stuff in that box is a secret. Don't you go blabbing it around, get it?"

"I didn't *blab* anything. I just asked a question."

"You were going to blab if Gideon hadn't left."

"Was not."

"Were too."

"Look, Tina, no point in arguing. The neat thing is that we might have had George Washington Carver's knife. The one he saw in the dream."

Tina's angry frown faded. "Looks like it."

"Pretty cool."

"Yes, and that's not the end of it. We have to get that box back."

"Let's hope we find the antique guy in Blue Eye."

They started back toward the Visitor Center.

"Want to look at the cool stuff in the museum?" Duncan asked.

"Absolutely not. I want to get home and check for ticks. Ticks freak me out!"

SIX

Bunny Suit

The Sheets-Ng Investigative Agency left for Silver Dollar City at seven o'clock in the morning. Not early enough. Long lines of traffic awaited Duncan, Tina, and Professor Sheets when they arrived at the popular tourist destination. After thirty minutes of bumper-to-bumper traffic, they finally parked at the far end of Lot Three, the furthest from the entrance. They hopped a crowded shuttle to the ticket booth. The driver told one corny joke after another, causing Professor Sheets and Duncan to laugh along with the other passengers. Tina rolled her eyes.

Thousands of people packed the streets of Silver Dollar City making it difficult to move and jostling Tina beyond annoyance. One of the biggest attractions turned out to be Professor Sheets himself who morphed into a giant kid. He rode every adult ride except Outlaw Run, the massive and terrifying wood roller coaster that towered over Silver Dollar City. Powdered sugar from a funnel cake the size of a garbage can lid dusted his too-tight Florida State University tee shirt. Professor Sheets couldn't wait to be photographed with his arms around two saucy dancers from the Saloon Show. He peppered the glass blower, blacksmith, and broom maker with questions about their ancient crafts. This drove

Duncan and Tina a little crazy. Late in the morning, they visited the wood carving shop. Professor Sheets became so excited by what he saw that he purchased a beginner's wood carving kit.

"Good grief," Duncan said, whispering to Tina. "Not another *two-day wonder*."

"What's that mean?" Tina asked.

"My dad is *such* an odd duck. He gets excited about something and decides it will be his new thing. It lasts about two days. My mom has a trunk full of stuff she calls *two-day wonders*. Inside the trunk there are books on writing novels, a beginner's harmonica kit, lousy paint-by-number canvasses, calligraphy pens, and a half-finished needlepoint of a horse. Mark my word. The carving kit will join the other two-day wonders. It drives my mom nuts."

Tina giggled.

By noon, Duncan, Tina, and Professor Sheets wearied of the long lines, whining kids, and occasional rudeness. The hot sun and high humidity made it miserable by mid-day. Time to leave. All three admitted to nervous excitement about what lay ahead for the Sheets-Ng Investigative Agency.

"Okay, team. Here's the plan," Professor Sheets said with a raised forefinger and a conspiratorial wink of his right eye. "When we get to Blue Eye, we'll begin by casing the joint."

Tina looked at Duncan and mouthed the words *casing the joint.*

Duncan shrugged his shoulders and held his arms out, palms up.

"My guess is this antique mall has lots of little booths," Professor Sheets continued, wiggling his forefinger. "We'll split up and look for this guy with slicked-down black hair and a black mustache. Let's call him *Slick.* If we see him, we won't do anything until we meet up and put our heads together. Got it?"

"Yessir," Duncan said.

Since Blue Eye had fewer than two hundred permanent residents, the Agency had no trouble locating the giant antique mall. The black wooden sign above the porch read, in gothic white letters, *Dead People's Rejects.* Two white skull and cross-bone images had been painted on each end of the sign.

"That name creeps me out," Duncan said.

"Me too," Tina said. "The skull and crossbones remind me of the pirate flag."

"Well. This guy we're looking for *is* a pirate."

"Okay, team, let's go," Professor Sheets said, brushing the powdered sugar off his tee shirt. "Remember, you two to the right. I'll go to the left. If we see Slick, we'll hook up again and decide the course to take. Roger that?"

Duncan rolled his eyes. "Roger that, Dad." He looked at Tina and shook his head.

The inside of Dead People's Rejects overwhelmed Tina and Duncan. To their immediate right stood a large L-shaped counter with a dozen customers waiting to pay. Four little old ladies worked feverishly to wrap glassware in old newspapers, ring up sales, and comment with little *oohs* and *ahs* over somebody's precious choice. As they surveyed the mall, Duncan and Tina could see aisle after aisle fifty yards in both directions. Aisles led to more aisles, which led to more aisles. *Casing the joint* was a big project.

"We could get totally lost in here," Tina said.

"No kidding," Duncan said.

"Stay together," Professor Sheets said. "Keep your eyes open for the guy and for the box. Let's meet back here in twenty minutes."

Tina and Duncan coursed up and down the aisles, peering into the many cluttered booths. Now and then, something would catch their eye like the big pink bunny suit they saw hanging in a booth filled with costumes.

"That's just like the suit Ralphie wore in the movie, *A Christmas Story*," Duncan said, fingering the rabbit ears sprouting from the feet. Tiny black button eyes stared up from below the ears.

"I didn't see that movie," Tina said.

"It's an old timer," Duncan said, "but funny. The kid in it is named Ralphie and his Aunt Clara made him a suit like this for Christmas. His mom made him wear it on Christmas morning. He looked really dumb."

"I'll bet," Tina said. "We better keep going."

Twenty minutes later, Tina and Duncan returned to the front counter to check in with Professor Sheets. He was nowhere to be found. They waited another ten minutes before going in search of him. It didn't take long. They spotted him in a booth filled with antique books. He stood browsing through an old volume, completely unaware of the time.

"Dad!" Duncan said with obvious irritation his voice.

"Wha? Oh… Duncan. What time is it?"

"You were supposed to meet us."

"Oh, yes… Sorry. I found this wonderful booth and lost track of the time. Did you see him?"

"No, but we didn't finish looking."

"Okay, okay. Let's keep looking. I'll tear myself away from this booth. Let's meet up twenty minutes from now in the front."

"Fine, Dad, but please be there this time."

"I will. I promise," Professor Sheets said with a sheepish little grin under his loopy mustache.

Duncan just shook his head and led Tina away to continue their search. Twenty minutes later they completed their exploration. No Slick, no box. When they reconnected with Professor Sheets, he reported the same outcome. Nothing.

"Dad," Duncan said. "Why don't we ask one of those clerks if Slick is here?"

Professor Sheets' eyebrows shot up and his jaw dropped. He sucked in a deep breath. "What a capital idea!" he said. "Why didn't I think of that?"

Duncan and Tina watched as Professor Sheets raced over to the counter and snagged the attention of a blue-haired clerk. Five seconds later, she shook her head.

"As luck would have it, he's not here today. He's on a buying trip." Professor Sheets said when he rejoined Duncan and Tina.

"What are we going to do?" Tina asked.

"We will have to come back," Professor Sheets said.

"But when?"

"Good question. I must review my calendar."

"All this way for nothing," Duncan said. "Bummer."

"Yes, yes it is," Professor Sheets agreed. Then his eyes brightened. "Well…maybe not. Say, kids, do you suppose you could find something to do for fifteen more minutes? There is this one book I saw…"

"Sure, Dad, fifteen minutes, and…maybe you could get us an ice cream cone on the way home?"

"Deal. I'll meet you at the car in fifteen," Professor Sheets said and scurried off toward the booth with the antique books.

"Another two-day wonder?" Tina asked.

"No, not with books. If my dad finds a book, he will read it for sure. He might read it more than once. My dad's a real bulldog with old books."

"What do you want to do?"

"Well, did you see that office in the back with the door cracked open?"

Tina nodded.

"Let's check it out. That might be Slick's office. Maybe we'll find a clue."

"Why not?" Tina said.

The two raced down several aisles toward the back of the building. When they shot out of the maze of booths, the office door loomed before them. They looked both right and left. A few wandered out of the aisles but none of them paid any attention to two kids.

"You stand guard, Duncan. I'll slip into the office."

"Okay but hurry. This makes me nervous."

"Don't be such a wuss. The guy isn't even here."

"But what if he returns from his buying trip?"

"Then warn me he's coming."

"Okay but hurry."

Tina ducked low and eased the door to the office open. It creaked, raising the hair on Duncan's neck. Ten seconds later, Tina whipped out of the office and came face-to-face with Duncan. He could feel her breath on his chin.

"It's in there," she said.

"The box?"

"Yes."

"What should we do?"

"Snatch it and run."

"How would we do that? They'll see us taking it. It might set off an alarm. I saw security cameras."

Tina nodded. "I hadn't thought of all that. But...we have to get the box."

Both of them stood there for several long seconds, trying to devise a plan of action.

Several heart beats later, Duncan's eyes brightened. "I know," he said.

"You know what?"

"The bunny suit."

"The bunny suit?"

"Yup, we'll buy the bunny suit and hide the box in it."

This time, Tina's eyes brightened.

"Do you remember how much the suit cost?" Duncan asked.

"I think the sign said ten dollars. It's a rip-off."

Duncan pulled out his little zippered wallet decorated with a Superman logo in red, yellow, and blue beads. "I've got five dollars. You have anything?"

Tina reached into the pocket of her lime green shorts and grasped a wad of bills. She counted them. "Me, too. I have five dollars."

"That won't be enough if they charge tax."

"Let's see if they'll take pity on us," Duncan said. "Maybe they'll sell it for ten bucks and let it go at that."

"Worth a try," Tina said.

It took five minutes to find the booth where they'd seen the bunny suit. They grabbed it off the rack and ran to the front counters.

"Oh how cute!" one of the little old lady clerks said when Duncan plopped the pink bunny suit on the counter. "Which one of you will be wearing it?"

Tina pointed toward Duncan.

Duncan pointed toward Tina.

The clerk laughed. "Well, I'm sure whoever wears it will be just darling."

Both children rolled their eyes.

"That will be ten dollars and eighty cents," The clerk said as she stuffed the bunny costume in a black plastic bag imprinted with white skull and crossbones.

"Uh, we only have ten dollars," Duncan said. "Would you take just ten dollars for it?"

"Well, I don't know."

"Here's eighty cents," came a voice from behind them.

Tina and Duncan turned to see a skinny old guy in a green John Deere hat. He held out eighty cents in his gnarled hand.

"Loved the movie," the old guy said. He poked Duncan's shoulder. "You look a little like Ralphie. Suit should look good on you."

Tina stifled another giggle.

A *little like Ralphie*? Duncan swallowed his pride and thanked the old guy. With black sack in hand, Duncan drew Tina into an unoccupied booth. "We've got about five minutes to go," he said stripping the bag off the bunny suit and discarding it on the floor. "Let's get the box."

They slipped into the office unnoticed, unzipped the bunny suit and spread it out on the floor atop a woven green scatter rug. As Duncan stood to retrieve the box from the desk, Tina felt around under her knees. "There's something under here," she said, peeling back the rug. "It's a trap door. Wonder what's down there."

"Tina! We don't have time for trap doors."

Ignoring Duncan, Tina lifted the trap door to reveal a ladder plunging into a darkened cellar. In a flash, she skittered down the rungs of the ladder.

"Tina!"

"Settle down, Duncan. I just want to see what's down here."

"What is it with you and cellars? Get up here before we get caught."

"There's a door leading somewhere…"

"Tina!"

"O-KAY!"

Two minutes later, Tina and Duncan walked out of *Dead People's Rejects* carrying the bunny suit and displaying the most innocent expressions they could muster. Professor Sheets sat behind the wheel of the minivan with his nose in the antique book he had just purchased. Duncan and Tina jumped in the back seat and held the bunny suit across their laps.

"What did you guys buy?" Professor Sheets said, laying his book aside and turning to look over the front seat of the car.

Duncan opened the zipper of the pink bunny suit.

"You found the box!" Professor Sheet said.

"Yup."

"Where?"

"In the guy's office."

"Everything there?"

"Haven't looked."

Professor Sheets hopped up on his knees in the front seat and leaned his head way into the back seat. "Well, let's have a look."

Duncan unlatched the lid of the box and raised it. A brief inspection of the contents confirmed that everything was still in place except, of course, the wallet.

"You know, kids, what you just did is theft."

"How can we steal what is ours?" Duncan asked.

"It's complicated," Professor Sheets said. "You see, Isaac Beiler thought he sold something he had a right to sell. Slick didn't think he was buying stolen property. Legally, I think he can claim he has a right to the box."

"But it's ours!" Tina said.

"I know. I know. I'm torn here kids. If we call the cops, they will take the box as evidence and there will be a long legal battle over it. Slick is going to fight tooth and toenail to keep the box. He knows what it is worth. Besides, the Amish guy is the biggest culprit, if there is a culprit. As I said before, I don't want to call the cops on peaceable Amish people."

"What if we bought it back from Slick?" Duncan asked.

"Okay, I can go with that. I'm sure Slick won't sell it. He knows what it's worth."

"No, I mean let's just leave him a hundred dollars and take off. Do you have a hundred dollars in your wallet, Dad?"

"Let me check." Professor Sheets thumbed the bills in his wallet. "Ah, I have one hundred and thirty dollars. Why don't I leave it all with the old ladies. That way he has the money he spent on the box plus a thirty dollar profit."

"Cool," Duncan said "but don't forget the ice cream."

"Ah yes, the ice cream. Let's go with a twenty percent profit. I'll keep ten dollars for ice cream."

Professor Sheets rummaged around in the glove box and found an old envelope. He sealed the money in it and scrawled *For the Manager* on the front. He jumped out of the car and raced into Dead People's Rejects. Ten eye blinks later, he returned and the Sheets-Ng Investigative Agency sped home.

SEVEN

Bushwhackers

Professor Sheets took immediate charge of the box, informing Duncan and Tina that nothing would be done until after school the next day.

"Aww, come on, Dad. Can't we just thumb through the stuff."

"Nope, not until tomorrow."

"Come on, Dad."

"Duncan... " A forbidding little frown creased Professor Sheets forehead. He lowered his voice. He meant business.

"Yes, sir," Duncan said, taking the hint. He hurried Tina outside for a game of lawn darts.

"This is dumb," Tina said.

"What's dumb?"

"Waiting to look at the box and playing dumb lawn darts."

Duncan handed her two lawn darts, the red ones. "You throw first."

~~~

The next day at school was the slowest on record. At the final bell, Tina and Duncan scampered into their school bus and sat on the edge of the front seat behind the driver. At the third bus stop, they blasted out of the doors and raced to the Sheets' house. Duncan came in second but his effort drew a touch of praise from Tina, "You might be getting faster." They needn't have hurried, however, because Professor Sheets didn't arrive until a full hour later.

"Where've you been, Dad? We've been waiting *forever*."

Professor Sheets glanced at his watch. "My, my. Forever is shorter than I thought. I didn't know forever lasted only an hour."

"Okay, okay, Dad. Let's get to the box."

They gathered around the old oak kitchen table. Mrs. Sheets joined them with a tray of glasses and pitcher of ice tea.

"Let's hold off on the ice tea, dear," Professor Sheets said. "We can't take the chance of spilling on the contents of the box."

"Of course," she said. "I'll set them on the counter here until we are finished."

Professor Sheets reached into the pocket of his rumpled, tweedy sports jacket. He pulled out three sets of white cotton gloves. "I borrowed these from the Newton County Historical Museum. Here, put them on."

"Why?" Tina asked. "These don't fit. They're dumb."

"Well, our fingers have oil on them, Tina. Natural oil our bodies produce. Plus, unless we've washed our hands thoroughly, we will have stuff on them, stuff we can't even see. The oils and particles on our fingers will damage historic documents so we must be careful when handling them."

Tina pursed her lips and twisted them to the side. She said nothing.

Professor Sheets raised the lid of the box. "Where shall we start?"

"We know about the knife," Duncan said. "Gideon explained Doctor Carver's spiritual nature and his dream regarding the knife."

"Well, I'll be!" Professor Sheets said. "That knife alone is worth the one hundred and twenty dollars we spent."

"I wanna see the letters," Tina said.

"Very well," Professor Sheets said. He jumped up and retrieved a clean white dishtowel from one of the kitchen drawers and spread it on the table. Hunching his shoulders three times to relieve the tension, he removed the packet of letters tied in a faded purple ribbon. After two more shoulder hunches, he held his breath and tugged one end of the bow. He did not allow himself to breathe until the circle of the bow had slid through the knot and the ribbon ends lay safely on the dishtowel. Professor Sheets looked at the others with his silly white-toothed smirk, flicked the right loop of his mustache, and corkscrewed his forefinger into the air. "Ta da!" he said. "The first letter."

Tina snaked her fingers toward the letters. Professor Sheets intercepted her hand and drew it aside. "Careful now," he said. "We'll read it in a minute but let's study it first. What catches your eye?"

Both children eased their heads forward until they were looking directly down on the letter. Mrs. Sheets peered over her husband's shoulder.

"It looks like it's been folded," Tina said.

"Yes, you can barely see the folds because it has been flattened for many years, but I agree, it was originally folded. What else can you see?"

"The paper is weird. It's like that paper we used in first grade. You know, the paper with fat lines."

"Yes, it's very rough paper. Anything else?"

"It appears torn on the edges and it's uneven on the sides," Mrs. Sheets said. "The top is narrower than the bottom."

"What might that tell us?" Professor Sheets asked.

"Maybe it was torn from a bigger piece of paper," Duncan said, wrinkling his forehead. "But why tear it?"

"Good question. Any ideas?"

"Maybe he didn't have a lot of paper and was saving some," Tina said.

"Good possibility," Professor Sheets said. "He was very poor. What do you think he used to write the letter?"

"Pencil," Tina and Duncan said in unison.

"Yes, pencil it is."

"Can we read it now? Please?" Duncan asked with an impatient whine.

"Yes we can." Professor Sheets picked up the rough-papered letter by the corners and held it in the palm of his hand. This is what they read.

Dear Jenie,

If you are reeding this letter, you been to the wonkie log and found it I am glad. I am fine here in nesho the school is helping me some and I can rite more as you can see I am staying with aunt marya and uncle andy they are negro folk and live next to the school they are good to me and take me to church but I have to work for them I am happy here but miss you jenie it was so kind of you and dangerous to be my friend a poor negro boy born into slave please put a letter in the wonkie log and when I come back to dimond grove I will get it.

love, carvers george

Slowly, the four readers looked up and stared at one another in silence.

"Oh my goodness," Professor Sheets said, his eyes wide and buggy. "Oh my goodness. Oh my goodness."

When he said it the third time and his eyes became buggier, a tiny alarm bell went off in Duncan's head. "Dad, you okay?"

Professor Sheets eased back in his chair and took a deep breath. His eyes were still buggy. "Oh, I'm *very* okay. Do you realize what we have here? If it is authentic, this is the earliest writing from the hand of George Washington Carver. When he was but a boy. I don't know much about his story. It's not a part of history I've studied, but I know this is huge. I mean really, really huge."

"Let's look at the rest of the letters," Tina said, bouncing in her chair like a wind-up toy.

"Oh, not yet, Tina. This letter tells us so much. Let's take our time. Take another look. What more does the letter tell us?"

"He can't spell very good," Duncan said.

"Right, he has spelling problems. I'm not sure how old he was when he wrote this. It appears he's just learning to write."

"No punctuation," Tina said.

"Right. He hasn't learned how to use periods, commas, or capital letters. What do you make of what he says?"

"Is *Jenie* the Jenny Jamison who owned this house?" Duncan

asked.

"It would seem so," Professor Sheets said. "Apparently they were close friends. Note he says it was dangerous for Jenny to befriend him. Why do you think?"

"'Cause he'd been a slave?" Tina wondered.

"Probably. I doubt if Jenny's parents would have wanted her to befriend a black boy."

"What's a wonkie log?" Mrs. Sheets asked.

Professor Sheets shrugged his shoulders. "No idea. Kids sometimes make up names for things. I wonder if this was a hollowed-out log that Jenny and George used as a secret mailbox."

Mrs. Sheets slipped into a chair. "I wonder who Aunt Marya and Uncle Andy were?"

"Again, I have no idea," Professor Sheets said.

"He signed the letter with the word *love* and I wonder why he called himself Carver's George," Duncan said.

"He may not have had a last name if he were born into slavery," Professor Sheets said. "Often slaves took the last name of the person who owned them. That must explain the name, *George Carver*. However, from this letter it appears that he hadn't taken that last name of Carver yet, or the middle name *Washington*, for that matter."

"Do you think he was in love with Jenny Jamison, Dad?"

"Eeeew," Tina said, scrunching up her nose as if she had just smelled dog doots. "Boyfriends and girlfriends are dumb. I'm never having a boyfriend."

Professor and Mrs. Sheets looked at each other with those smuggy parent smiles that seem to say, *we'll see.*

"He may have been in love with her," Professor Sheets said, "but it may have just been an expression of friendship. In those days, friendships were often described as loving relationships even if it weren't, you know, romantic love."

"He uses the word *negro*. I thought we weren't supposed to say that," Duncan said.

"Again, in those days the word *negro* was perfectly acceptable and used by good people in both races. It's only been in the last fifty years or so that we have found it better to use *black* or *African American.*"

"How can we find out more about this letter, Dad?"

"Well, I can do some research but I don't have much time with school starting."

"I bet Gideon could tell us a lot," Tina said.

"Oh, I'm sure he could."

"Can we go over to the Monument and talk to him tomorrow after school?" Duncan asked.

Professor Sheets looked at his wife with inquiring eyebrows.

"It's okay with me if you are home for dinner," she said.

"Very well, I think that's enough for today," Professor Sheets said, folding the purple ribbon back over the bundle of letters. "This evening I'll catalog these letters. And kids, when you talk to Gideon tomorrow, don't spill the beans about the box and letters. Eventually, we will have to turn them over to the Monument but we are in the midst of an historic discovery. We should enjoy it ourselves for a time. After all, we bought the box. It was included in the price of the house along with everything else in the basement. Besides, I smell a research paper on this historic find. Probably more than one."

~~~

"Well, if it isn't my good friends from the neighborhood," Gideon said as Tina and Duncan pushed through the front door of the Visitor Center at the Monument. "Are you here for more stories?"

"Uh, maybe. But we have some questions first. Can we ask you some questions?"

"Of course. Let's go into the theater. They won't show the film for twenty minutes. No one else will be in there."

"So, what are your questions?" Gideon asked when they seated themselves on benches in the dim light of the theater.

"We want to know when he was born, who his mom and dad were, how he got out of slavery, where he grew up and went to school, did he have any brothers and sisters, who are Aunt Marya and Uncle Andy, and what's a wonkie log?" Tina said, her words tumbling out of her mouth like marbles out of a bag.

"Whoa," Gideon said, holding up his hand and laughing at Tina's word blast. "One question at a time. Fair enough?"

Both children nodded.

Gideon stood with his back to the movie screen. Three can lights created a soft glow and when Gideon stood, he appeared as a silhouette against the movie screen, his face barely visible. He raised his arms, as he often did when telling a story, and resembled a monster from a scary old black-and-white movie.

"All right," he said, leaning forward as if to tell a secret. "I want you to close your eyes and picture this in your mind's eye." Gideon's voice lowered to a soft purr. "Moses Carver and his wife Susan had just settled down after a long day on the farm. Dark and moonless came the night, soundless save for choirs of cicadas and the occasional *bumm-bumm* bullfrog bellowing from Carver Creek.

"Suddenly, thundering horse hooves pounded away the silence. Moses jumped to his feet and stole a glance out the window. 'Bushwhackers, Susan! Quick to the brush pile! I'll warn Mary.' 'Not again!' Susan screamed, leaping from her chair and racing from the house. Moses Carver followed her hollering to his slave woman, 'Mary, Bushwhackers! Run!' He plowed into the slave cabin, scooped up George's brother Jim and lit out for a giant brush pile in the darkest end of the farmyard. They buried themselves in the thicket of branches and huddled into small balls.

"Mary dashed to the crib where George lay sleeping and drew him into her arms.

"Too late.

"A giant man filled the doorway of the slave cabin. 'And what have we here?' he said, his voice a deep, a menacing growl. 'A little slave mama and her pickaninny.' Before she could move, the giant man bear-hugged Mary and her baby, dragging them out of the cabin. He hauled them into the arms of another man who stood guarding the horses. The guard held Mary so tightly that she and George could barely breathe. She kept her silence for fear of betraying Moses, Susan, and Jim lying still as death in the brush pile.

"The Bushwhackers – three of them – stalked the farm in search of the Carvers and a stash of money the family had squirreled away. After thirty minutes of searching, the three rejoined the guard who guarded Mary. Mary trembled beneath the iron grip of the fourth Bushwhacker. Baby George, who had whooping cough, broke the silence with sharp barks from deep within his lungs.

"'No luck,' the big man said. 'Tore up the house. Cain't find nothin' and don't know where them Carvers got off to. Hidin' here abouts, but hidin' good.'

"Another man lit a thin cigar and blew out a stream of smoke. 'Best be movin' on,' he said. 'We'll take them slaves on down south of the Arkansas line. My man Ferrell will buy 'em, take 'em to Looziana and sell 'em there. Let's mount up boys. Come back another day. Get hold of that Carver. We got ways of makin' him talk.'"

Duncan and Tina sat spellbound by Gideon's story.

"What happened?" Tina asked, her voice a notch above a whisper.

Gideon nodded and took a deep breath. "Well, that's where the story gets even fuzzier, but I'll tell you what happened the way I see it. I figure Mary cradled her sick baby as she rode in front of the man with the iron grip. The horses ran at breakneck speed out of Missouri down into Confederate Arkansas. Bushwhackers, who sided with the South in the Civil War, found safety in Arkansas.

"Meanwhile, Moses Carver rode hard on one of his prize racehorses, through the moonless night, to John Bentley's adjoining farm. 'John,' Moses said, jumping off his horse, 'Bushwhackers got my Mary and the babe.'

"'When?' John asked, curling his thumb around a suspender.

"'Last night. Me, Sue, and the boy hid. Raiders couldn't find us.'

"'Probably headed south to sell 'em,' John said.

"'That's why I come to you,' Moses said. 'You know 'bout these raiding parties, where they hole up an' all. Figure you could go lookin' for Mary and the babe?'

"Bentley ran a hand through his long black hair and took a deep breath. 'Reckon I could,' he said.

"'Make it worth your while,' Moses said. 'This here gray racehorse is yours if you succeed. I've got forty acres right next to your place. I'll throw them in to boot, you bring 'em both back safe and sound. Mary's part of the family and the babe – we call him George – is a puny little thing but my Sue has taken a liking to him.'

"'That's a mighty fine horse,' Bentley said, nodding his head toward the animal. 'Course I could use another forty acres. Been wantin' to plant some Indian corn. I'll strike out for Arkansas at daybreak. See what I can find.'"

"Did he find them?" Duncan asked.

Gideon held up his hand. "Coming to that. It seems Bentley found the Bushwhacker camp. The baby George was there but Mary was nowhere to be found. Bushwhackers had no use for a runty baby, not likely to live anyway. Gave George up to Bentley without a squawk."

"What happened to her?" Tina asked.

"No one knows," Gideon said. "Some say she was sold into another slave home. Others say she made a break for freedom. Still others say she died of pneumonia. There have been some who claim she wound up in northern Missouri as a maid. No one has the final answer. When Bentley got the baby George back from the Bushwhackers and took him home, the poor thing lingered near death. Susan took him in her arms and nursed him back to health. The Carvers raised him as if he were one of their own. Bentley got the racehorse but refused the land because he failed to bring Mary back."

"Wow!" Duncan said. "That's a *stemwinder*. My dad always says that. But Gideon, what about George's father?"

"Again, we don't know," Gideon continued. "George himself thought his father was a slave owned by a neighbor. Apparently, this young slave man was killed in a logging accident. In any case, we know nothing more about George's father. So, the scrawny little boy grew up as an orphan. He had no memory of his parents. Can you imagine what that must have been like, growing up as an orphan?"

Silence filled the theater as Duncan and Tina tried to picture themselves without a mom and dad.

"But the Carvers took care of George, right?" Tina said, trying to shoo away the gloom.

"Yes, they did," Gideon said with a gentle smile. "Susan took good care of George, who was sickly throughout his childhood. Unlike his brother Jim, he wasn't strong enough to do much of the farm work. Instead, Susan taught him to cook, iron, sew, and weave. However, I don't think that's the whole story because later, as a young man, he had his own land. He knew how farm so he must have done some of the heavier work on the Carver place."

"So what about Aunt Marya and Uncle Andy?" Tina asked.

"Who were they?"

"Ah, come with me," Gideon said, rising from his bench.

He led the two children into one of the galleries in the museum. There, in a glass case, stood a mannequin in a long white dress with blue trim.

"That's Aunt Mariah's dress," Gideon said. "Here, next to the case, is a picture of her."

"She's pretty," Tina said, noting a different spelling of Marya.

"Yes, she was," Gideon said. "Come with me. Let me show you another picture."

Gideon walked a few feet and pointed to a yellowed picture on the wall just above Duncan's eye level. "George Washington Carver drew this many years after he left Missouri."

Tina and Duncan gazed at an excellent pencil sketch of two buildings. At the top left were the words *Aunt Mariah's home*. An arrow pointed to a small house with an outbuilding in the back. On the right, had been penciled the word, *School*, with an arrow pointing toward a smaller building.

"You see," Gideon said, "When George was perhaps twelve years old – we're not really sure how old – he took off for Neosho to attend the *colored school*. That's what they called African American people in those days – *colored*. Black and white kids couldn't go to school together and there was no colored school in Diamond Grove. Yet, George had such a powerful urge to learn that he walked eight miles from the Carver farm to Neosho. That first day, he wandered around town and finally found the school but couldn't find a place to stay. Night drew near, so he went to the house next door to the school, sneaked into that outbuilding, and slept in stacked hay.

Aunt Mariah discovered him the next morning sitting on a stump eating his sunflower seeds. Aunt Mariah struck up a conversation with George. After discovering why he was in her yard, she offered room and food in exchange for work. Aunt Mariah was quite famous in these parts. She was a midwife. Do you know what a midwife is?"

Tina and Duncan shook their heads.

"Well, midwives deliver babies. There were few doctors in southwest Missouri in those days. Ladies called midwives helped mothers to deliver their babies. Aunt Mariah not only worked as a midwife, we think she also trained as a nurse. She had been born into slavery and her owner was a doctor. He may have trained Mariah. She was skilled in the use of plants to heal various diseases. When parents went on vacation, Mariah cared for their children. Sometimes she taught the children to read and write. Certainly, she helped George with his schooling. Aunt Mariah and Uncle Andy made good money, and they were role models for George, showing him black people could be successful."

Tina and Duncan continued to stare at the drawing. As they did so, Duncan asked again if George Washington Carver knew Jenny Jamison. Gideon thought for a moment. "As I said earlier Jamison is a common name around here. George might have known a Jenny Jamison. Why do you ask?"

"She's the one who built our old house."

"Could be they knew each other, Duncan. I must look into that one. I'll browse the library and see if I can find out anything about a Jenny Jamison. Next time you come, I might have an answer for you."

"What's a wonkie log?" Tina asked.

"A wonkie log?"

"Yes, have you ever heard of a wonkie log?"

Gideon laughed. "No, I can't say I have. A wonkie log. That's a new one on me."

Eight

Tina's Troubles

Very odd, Duncan thought. Professor Sheets agreed. So did Mrs. Sheets. Tina had not come to visit since she and Duncan heard the *stemwinder* story of George Washington Carver's kidnapping. In fact, she hadn't shown up for the better part of a week. *Very odd*. Out of loyalty to his friend, Duncan told his father he wanted to wait before examining the other letters until Tina could be present. Professor Sheets found this acceptable. He was pressed into several evening meetings at Crowder College anyway and didn't have time to spend on the letters.

Gideon called two days later. Duncan had left his family cell phone number with Gideon in case he came up with something interesting. Mrs. Sheets was the first to hear the duck quack – the ring tone they had selected for the family cell phone. She made small talk before turning the phone over to Duncan.

"I've got information for you," Gideon said.

"What's that?" Duncan asked.

"It's about Jenny Jamison."

"Tell me."

"Well, she appears to have been born in eighteen sixty, a few years before George. Her mother and father hailed from Tennessee and came to Missouri hoping to find good land in a new place. That they did. They bought one hundred acres of land, cleared it, and built a productive farming operation, as good or better than Moses Carver's."

"So she knew George."

"Had to have known him. Though she was four or five years older than George, she would certainly have known him. I doubt they *hung out together*, as you kids say today, but she would have seen him around, maybe talked with him."

"Cool."

"So tell me, Duncan, aside from living in the old Jamison place, why are you so curious about Jenny?"

An alarm bell chimed in Duncan's brain. He remembered what his dad had said, *Don't spill the beans.* He shook his head to clear it causing the phone to crackle.

"Just curious," Duncan said. "Wanted to know more about the lady who owned our house."

"I see," Gideon said. "There is one other bit of information I discovered."

"Yeah?"

"Jenny's parents were killed in a carriage accident when she was eighteen. She inherited the farm and house. She ran it until she died herself in 1943, the same year George passed."

"Oh," Duncan said, not knowing how to respond.

An awkward silence followed. Finally, Gideon spoke. "I thought you might want to know these things, since you brought them up."

"Oh, yeah, for sure. Thanks Gideon. Good stuff."

"All right, Duncan, you have a good evening. You and Tina come by anytime."

"Yeah, sure, will do," Duncan said. "Bye Gideon."

"Bye, Duncan," Gideon said, a chuckle under his voice.

"So what was that all about?" Professor Sheets lowered his newspaper to a crumple in his lap.

"That was Gideon," Duncan said, repeating what his friend, the volunteer ranger, had discovered about Jenny Jamison.

"Well, that is interesting," Professor Sheets said, "and so is this." The front page of the *Neosho Daily News* displayed four photographs under the headline, *Crowder College Welcomes New*

Faculty Members. Three of the new teachers wore typical clothing in their pictures – casual shirts and blouses, no headwear. Not Professor Sheets. He sported an academic robe and one of those pillowy velvet hats that professors wear. His mustache loops seemed larger than usual, as did his grin. *Such an odd duck.* Looking over her husband's shoulder, Mrs. Sheets read the paragraph on her husband.

> *Professor Delbert Sheets comes to Crowder from his most recent position at the University of Miami. He holds a Bachelor's degree in history from Wabash College (Indiana) as well as a Masters and Doctorate in American History from Florida State University. His publication record is impressive with over forty journal articles in print. He is the author of* African American Contributions to the Building of Spanish Florida, *published by the University of Florida Press. Doctor Sheets won the prestigious* Teacher-Scholar Award *from the University of Miami.* "It is rare for Crowder to attract someone of Professor Sheets' academic stature," *said George Countryman, Chairman of the Social Sciences Division.* "We are indeed fortunate to have secured his services. It will no doubt elevate the reputation of Crowder College."

Reading these words took Duncan back to the family dinner table in Miami six months earlier. He had just chomped down on one of his mother's splendid chicken tacos when Professor Sheets announced that he had resigned from his position at the University of Miami. They were moving, heading to a new home in another state. Duncan couldn't believe his ears and looked up at his father with a mouth full of un-crunched tortilla shell. At last it all made sense. He remembered his father's unexplained trip to a secret place known only to his parents. There were the hushed conversations, momentarily stopped whenever he entered the room. Duncan hadn't forgotten the mysterious phone conversation, which concluded with Mrs. Sheets saying, "Yes, tomorrow morning would be fine for a bid on the contents of the house." Now over a taco dinner, his dad had *spilled the beans* – they were leaving Florida. Duncan narrowed his eyes. *Did mom fix my favorite dinner on purpose?*

"But where?" Duncan asked, mumbling around his mouthful.

"Southwest Missouri. I'm taking a position at Crowder College in a little city called Neosho."

"Southwest where?"

"Missouri."

"I don't know where that is."

"We'll show you on the map," Mrs. Sheets said, in the gentle voice that had always made Duncan feel safe. This time, he wasn't so sure.

"But why?"

Professor Sheets swallowed his own gob of taco and patted his mustache with a white paper napkin. "Your mother and I are not comfortable with life here in Miami anymore. There is a high crime rate and, as you know, right in our own quiet neighborhood there have been a string of burglaries and one drug-related murder. Also, I have a long commute. The traffic is not getting any lighter. We think it would be best for our family if we moved somewhere safer and less hectic."

"But what about all my friends, my school?"

"You'll make new friends and the school in our new town is better."

Duncan chewed his taco and stared at his father. After several long eye-to-eye seconds he asked, in a low voice, "Dad, did you get fired?"

Professor Sheets threw his head back and laughed. "No, no no. Nothing like that. Of course, all of my fellow faculty members think I'm completely nuts."

They're right, Duncan thought to himself. *You are completely off your rocker.*

As he thought more and more about the move, Duncan's emotions overcame him. He jumped up from the table and ran to his room. A minute later, his parents found him sitting on the edge of his bed on the verge of tears. Professor and Mrs. Sheets sat next to him and put their arms around his shoulders.

"I know it's tough, honey," Mrs. Sheets said, "but it is best for the family. And that's the most important thing in the world – our family."

"I don't understand why dad wants to leave this big university to teach in a place no one has ever heard of. And Dad's famous."

"Well, Duncan," Professor Sheets said, flicking a mustache loop, "I wouldn't call me famous. The good Lord has given me the gift of teaching. There are many students in Missouri with whom I could share that gift. That's what I think the good Lord is calling me to do."

"But Dad, you can't make as much money there."

"Money isn't everything, son. We've never made money the most important thing in life. I assure you, we will make enough to live comfortably. I've bought an old house in a little town outside Neosho. It's called Diamond. I got the house for next to nothing. It's a *fixer-upper* but it is out in the country – beautiful country. Safe. You can ride your bike all around, something we can't let you do here. It's just not safe anymore."

It took several weeks for Duncan to get used to the idea of moving but, over the course of that summer, excitement grew. Each step along the way – selling the house, a successful garage sale, packing his room, watching the moving van load up, and finally jumping in the car for a 1,400 mile trip increased Duncan's sense of adventure. A promised stop at Disney World further perked his anticipation. Then, upon arrival Duncan saw the old dilapidated house his father had bought. His enthusiasm rolled away like an ebb tide on the Atlantic Ocean, not far from his old house. He already missed his old house more than he could have imagined.

So, when Tina popped up on his doorstep two days after moving into the old Jamison place, Duncan felt a wave of relief. Prickly though she could be, Tina was a sight for Duncan's homesick eyes. And now, she had become his best friend. His only friend. Thinking about Tina thrust Duncan back to the present moment and he wondered again, *where has she been*? She hasn't been by the house in five days. He'd seen her in school but every time he tried to talk to her, she scooted away. Had he said or done something to upset her?

Another day passed and then, to the relief of everyone, Tina banged on the Sheets' front door. When Duncan opened the door, Tina burst into the house and buried herself in Mrs. Sheets' apron where she dissolved into uncontrolled sobbing. Mrs. Sheets held her while Duncan stared in awkward silence. Finally, Tina's tearful eruption subsided. Mrs. Sheets put her hands on Tina's shoulders, moved her a few inches away, and stooped to look into her eyes.

"Tina, honey, what's the trouble?"

Tina glanced at Duncan and gave her head a little shake.

"Ah," Mrs. Sheets murmured and turned to her son, "Duncan, sweetie, would you be so good as to go make a pitcher of lime Kool Aid and there are double stuffed Oreos in the cupboard. Why don't you get those out as well? Tina and I will be a minute. Recognizing a pending *girl talk*, Duncan turned on his heel and ambled into the kitchen.

Mrs. Sheets drew Tina into the living room where they sat on the big green couch.

"Can you tell me what's wrong, Tina?"

She sniffle-nodded. "It's been bad at my house. My daddy lost his job at the toothpaste factory. I don't know why. Something about *downsizing.* And Tonya's gone."

"Who's Tonya?"

"She's my big sister. She's a druggie."

"A druggie?"

"Yeah. She didn't used to be, but she started hanging out with these Goth kids in high school. She went Goth too. These kids were into drugs, weed, cheese, you know."

"No, dear, I don't. What is cheese?"

"You snort it. It's got heroin in it, I don't know."

Tina crossed her legs and wrapped her arms around herself. Mrs. Sheets put her arm over Tina's shoulders and drew her close. "Do your parents know?"

"Yeah, they've tried to get her help, but she doesn't want it. Then, day before yesterday, Tonya almost died. She overdosed. My folks decided she had to go into big-time treatment. Today my dad took Tonya to Tulsa to a rehab center. She'll live there until she is well... If she gets well."

"What about your mom? Can you talk to her about it?"

Tina shrugged. "My mom is old Chinese. She's ashamed and she won't talk about it."

"I see," Mrs. Sheets said. "Do you think it helps to talk about it?"

Tina nodded.

"Good. You can talk to me if you wish. Anytime. We shall pray that Tonya gets better and is home soon."

"I won't pray."

"Why not?"

"I don't believe in God. My dad says there is no God."

"Well, then, is it okay if I pray for Tonya?"

"Won't do any good."

"We'll see, honey. Now, how about some Kool Aid and cookies."

Tina nodded and looked up at Mrs. Sheets. "Thanks, Mrs. Sheets," she said.

Mrs. Sheets offered a motherly smile. As they walked toward the kitchen, she said, "Do you want me to keep this a secret from Duncan?"

"You can tell him… Only after I leave."

"All right. Before we go into the kitchen, let me see your face."

Mrs. Sheets rubbed her thumb under Tina's eyes to wipe away the dried tear crumbs.

~~~

Stomping into the kitchen like a Prussian corporal, Tina snatched an empty glass from of Duncan's hand. She poured herself a brimming glass of Kool Aid and downed it in one gulp. She ran over to the package of Oreos, tore it open, and shoved a whole Double Stuffed into her mouth. Duncan gave his mother a curious glance. Mrs. Sheets gave a tiny shake of her head.

Taking the hint, Duncan poured Tina another glass of Kool Aid and prepared the plate of Oreos. "So, my Dad will be home soon," he said. "Maybe we can look at another letter."

Tina shrugged as if to say, *whatever.*

As if on cue, the front door creaked open. Professor Sheets tromped down the hallway and into the kitchen. He piled his tweedy sport coat and ratty leather briefcase on the counter. He pulled a glass from the cupboard. "That Kool Aid looks *scrumpdili-ishus* on a hot September day. Mind if I have some?"

"Sure, Dad, I'll pour." *Scrupdili-ishus?*

The four of them sat around the table drinking lime Kool Aid and devouring Double Stuffed Oreos. Professor Sheets asked that typically unproductive question, *how was school today?* Tina and Duncan shrugged. After equally unproductive questions about math, English, social studies, and science, Professor Sheets finally offered to look at another letter. Both children nodded though Tina's enthusiasm was subdued.

Rubbing his hands together in gleeful anticipation, Professor Sheets directed his two children to *clear the decks.* He ran up the stairs – two at a time – to retrieve the precious box from his office.

"I've catalogued these letters," he said. "There are thirty-four of them beginning with last week's. George Washington Carver wrote the last letter two weeks before he died. All of them are to Jenny Jamison. Some of them are *very* interesting. I've picked one out I think we should look at.

They slipped on the white gloves and placed the letter on a clean white dishtowel. Professor Sheets, sensing that Tina had suffered some misfortune in her life, asked her to read its contents. He hoped by reading the letter, her mind could be drawn away from her troubles, at least for a few minutes. In a small voice that grew stronger with each sentence, Tina read:

> *124 West Second Street*
> *Minneapolis, Kansas*
> *August 24, 1881*

My dear Jenny,

I am home in Minneapolis with Ben and Lucy Seymour. You remember me telling you about them. They are like parents to me. I am back at my washing and ironing. My school begins in a few days and I am eager to return to my studies. I think I shall start Latin. It is nice to be home in Minneapolis because it has been a good town for me, a pleasant place after the horrors of Fort Scott and the difficulties of Paola. Olathe was safe but the Old Stone School did not meet my expectations.

Though it is good to be home, I must tell you how much I miss you. I had a delightful time with you when I returned to Diamond Grove this past summer. As I told you, I remain sorry about the loss of your folks but it was good to visit inside your house and not in secret by the Wonkie Log. It is such a beautiful house and we had a grand time, did we not, talking about this and that, drinking tea, and munching on those wonderful biscuits of yours. Thank you again for the recipe. I shall try it on the Seymours before long.

Do write to me at the above address when you have a moment. I long to read your letters and shall treasure them forever. Perhaps I can return to Diamond Grove next year. Pray for me as I shall for you.

With much love and affection,

George

"Holy cow!" Duncan said. "So George Washington Carver was in this house as a kid, a teenager."

"He sure was," Professor Sheets said. "And it was a beautiful house."

"Not so much anymore," Duncan said flatly.

"Patience, Duncan, we will bring it back to its former gorgeousness in due time."

Duncan wondered if *gorgeousness* were an actual word but decided not to raise the question. There were more important questions to ask. What were the horrors of Fort Scott? The difficulties in Paola? The problems with the Old Stone School? Professor Sheets could not answer these questions but suggested Tina and Duncan check with Gideon after school the following day. "Be sure you think carefully about your questions to Gideon so you don't spill the beans."

Duncan couldn't help but smile and, for just a split second, he thought he saw a fleeting smile on Tina's lips as well.

NINE

Death on the Dresden

Gideon drew Tina and Duncan into the Monument theatre to answer questions arising from the letter they had recently examined. He didn't perform a dramatic story telling this time but presented the information in a matter-of-fact way.

"Yes, George opened a washing and ironing business in several towns. He needed to earn enough money for his room, board, and education. He wandered from place-to-place in his late teens and early twenties. In one town, Fort Scott, Kansas, he had a terrifying experience. He witnessed the hanging of a black man by a mob of white people. It so horrified him he left the town immediately. He claimed the memory of that lynching haunted him to his dying day. We know little about his stay in Paola but he must not have found it a favorable city because he didn't stay long. In Olathe, he attended school but, again, it must not have been to his liking. So, he wound up again with the Seymours who had moved to Minneapolis, Kansas. The Seymours had always treated him as if he were their own child. He liked Minneapolis, Kansas where he completed his upper elementary and high school subjects."

Gideon paused and looked at Duncan and Tina out of the corner of his eyes, his curiosity mounting. "You two seem to have learned a great deal about Doctor Carver since last we spoke. Where are you getting this information?"

Tina and Duncan looked at each other. "We've been reading," Duncan said.

"I see," Gideon said, a trace of suspicion lingering in his voice. "Well, to be sure, he led an interesting life, especially in the early years."

"Did he ever come back to Diamond Grove," Tina asked.

"Yes, several times as he got older. The earliest time on record was 1884. His writings hint he may have returned earlier but we have no proof."

"Actually…" Tina said, bouncing on the bench.

"Beans!" Duncan shouted. "Beans!"

"Woops." She clamped her hand over her mouth.

"Beans?" Gideon said with a puzzled look.

"Yes, beans," Duncan said. "I love beans, don't you Tina? I wonder if George Washington Carver liked beans."

Gideon looked at Duncan as if he had gone barmy. "Beans? That's an odd question."

Scrambling to recover, Duncan nodded. "Yes, beans. We know he was interested in peanuts and chickpeas. Just wondered about beans."

Gideon shook his head. "I'm not sure about beans."

With that, Duncan nudged Tina and announced that they should head home. Once they were on their bikes and racing from the Monument, Duncan called to Tina, riding in front. "What's the matter with you, Tina? You nearly spilled the beans."

"Did not!"

"Yes you did and you know it. Gideon is getting suspicious. We need to cool it for a while."

"He doesn't know about the letters. How could he?"

"That's not the point. We can't have him getting too suspicious. We don't know what will happen. Slick might call the cops or something. Then we could be under investigation. Gideon would be called to testify."

"That's dumb. You worry too much."

"You don't worry enough!"

"Drop it Duncan. Nothing's going to happen."

~~~

The following Sunday dawned with a bright blue sky and much cooler temperatures. A high-pressure front had moved through southwest Missouri sweeping away the heat and humidity. As the Sheets family drove to Calvary Presbyterian Church, Mrs. Sheets explained the sad circumstances in Tina Ng's family. "We should pray for them," she said. Both Duncan and Professor Sheets nodded in agreement.

Unlike most children, Duncan enjoyed church. He loved the old hymns much more than contemporary choruses. He found the lyrics ancient and meaningful. In the matter of hymns, he wished his father would mouth the words. He couldn't carry a tune in a washtub. On any number of occasions, Mrs. Sheets had said, "Delbert, dear, softly... please, softly." The professor responded by assuring his wife that when the notes arrive in heaven they are beautiful to God's ears. "Yes," she would say, "But for those of us left here on earth, they are not yet ready for God's ears. So... softly, please."

Duncan listened carefully to the sermons. Mostly, he could follow Pastor Covington and often engaged his parents in conversation about points in the sermon. The other kids traipsed off to Sunday School when it came time for the sermon. They much preferred the dumbed-down Bible stories and artsy-craftsy projects to the *dry* sermons. Not Duncan. He wanted the real stuff dished out to adults. This strange preference caused Duncan to wonder, from time-to-time, if he were an odd duck in the making. Perhaps this acorn hadn't fallen too far from the old oak tree. However, Duncan vowed he would never wear a red-checked shirt and orange bow tie, such as his father sported on this Sunday morning.

There came a time in the church service when people named aloud those for whom their prayers were desired. At that moment, Duncan blurted, "Dear God, I pray for my friend Tina's sister and her dad." A hush followed. No one in the congregation could remember a child offering such a petition. Embarrassed, Duncan lowered his head and tried to form himself into a tiny ball. As other names were loosened from the lips of those in the congregation, Duncan's mother put a hand on his knee and patted him. When they left the church, Pastor Covington gave Duncan a good rub on the carrot top, praising him for his courage.

Later that afternoon, Tina hammered on the Sheets' front door, momentarily arresting the deafening snore thundering from Professor Sheets' slackened jaw. He lay sprawled on the old green couch, one foot on the coffee table and his hands clasped under the bib of his overalls. The bib overalls were a sore point in the family. Upon arriving in the Ozarks, Professor Sheets hurried to the farm supply store where he bought two pairs of blue bib overalls. When he first modeled them, after work one afternoon, Mrs. Sheets put her hands on her hips and said, "Oh no you don't! Not in my house. You look like a backwoods hillbilly." To this Professor Sheets proudly declared, "I am a backwoods hillbilly. At least I am now."

They went round and round. Duncan scurried outside to pitch lawn darts until things cooled. When he re-entered the house, peace reigned once more. His parents had reached a truce. Professor Sheets could wear the bib overalls around the house, but never, ever in public. Ever. They must have been comfortable overalls and quite suitable for a nap on this warm Sunday afternoon.

"Want to look at another letter?" Duncan whispered as he closed the front door.

Tina nodded but wondered, "Do we dare wake your dad up?"

"He won't care. Come on. This could be funny."

Duncan led Tina on tiptoes to the side of the couch. He flicked his father's mustache loops. After several flicks, Professor Sheets stopped snoring and wrinkled his nose as if he had an itch. Tina and Duncan writhed in silent laughter. Duncan put his finger to his lips to assure silence and then performed a few double flicks on both sides of the mustache. Professor Sheets wriggled his nose again and withdrew his hand from under his overall bib to swipe at an imaginary insect. The children couldn't contain their giggles and when they burst out in laughter, Professor Sheets opened one eye. He rubbed his nose.

"What's up?" he said.

Duncan sobered, but still smiling, asked if they could examine another letter. With considerable effort, Professor Sheets drew himself up into a sitting position. "Why sure," he said. "But I have an idea. Why don't we look at that other letter, the one from Rudolf Diesel?"

"But it's in German. Can you read the German, Dad?"

"I think so. I might have to look up a word or two, but I think I can get through it. What do you say?"

"Okay by me," Duncan said. "You okay with it, Tina?"

Tina nodded.

With hands in white gloves they opened the letter and Professor Sheets began his translation of the German. "The letter was written from the *Hotel Metropole* in Brussels, Belgium. The date is September 28, 1913. This is what it says:

My Dear Professor Carver:

I wish to thank you for your recent work on the use of peanut oil as a diesel fuel. It appears very promising. We will have to determine how best to extract the oil, refine it, and deliver it. It can become the low-cost fuel we both desire. Your work on developing a non-edible peanut that is high in oil is exciting. It may be the solution. As you have noted, peanuts produce much more oil per acre than do soy beans."

Professor Sheets paused in his reading. "Does this make sense to you?" he asked Tina and Duncan. Both nodded and urged him to continue.

"I did so enjoy meeting you in America this past spring. Thank you for arranging to meet in the little village of Diamond, far from cities and newspaper reporters. My work often brings unwanted attention and our time in the countryside was not only enlightening, it gave me time to relax. I so appreciated Fraulein Jamison's hospitality.

"I hope to live long enough to see the fruits of your labors in behalf of diesel technology. However, I must disclose to you I fear for my life. I leave on the morrow for England. I am to attend the ground-breaking of a new diesel plant in Ipswich. From there I will go to London where I will give a speech to the Royal Automobile Club. While in England, I will meet with Sir Winston Churchill, First Lord of the Admiralty..."

Here Professor Sheets stopped his reading once again. "Do you know who Winston Churchill was?" he asked.

"Of course," Tina said, crossing her arms. "He was an English leader. Everybody knows that."

Duncan stared at his shoes.

"Very good, Tina," Professor Sheets said, adopting his history professor voice. "He was the Prime Minister of England during World War Two. Some say without his leadership, the Germans would have won the war. He was an amazing leader during a desperate time for England. But..." Professor Sheets held up his professor finger. " Did you know that in 1913, he was First Lord of the Admiralty, which meant he was in charge of the English Navy?"

Duncan and Tina shook their heads.

"That's important here. Listen to what Rudolf Diesel writes. Professor Sheets turned his eyes to the letter.

Sir Winston wants me to share my most recent improvements on submarine engines. As you know, war with England is pending and my government is fearful that I might provide technical secrets to the English, giving them an advantage when war comes. I have had men – I can only assume they are German agents – shadowing me, following me wherever I go. I have no doubt there will be German agents aboard the Dresden *when we cross the North Sea from Antwerp, Belgium to Harwich, England. So, if you do not hear from me again, you will know what happened. My very best to you.*

"Signed *Rudolf Diesel.*"

Professor Sheets looked up from the letter and gazed at the ceiling.

"What's the matter, Dad?" Duncan asked.

"Trying to remember. If my memory serves, I don't think Rudolf Diesel made it to England. Hang on a second."

Despite his ample size, Professor Sheets jumped from the couch and raced into the kitchen. Duncan wondered if the bib overalls had given him a boost in agility and speed. When the professor returned, breathless, he punched a number on his cell phone. He put the phone on *Speaker* and set it on the coffee table. "Calling a history colleague at Crowder," Professor Sheets said in a soft voice. After five rings, a deep voice sounded through the phone.

"Hooper here."

"Carl," Professor Sheets said, "Delbert here. Sorry to bother you on a Sunday. Since you are an expert in the history of technology during the Twentieth Century, I've got a question for you."

"Shoot," Professor Hooper said.

"Do you know how Rudolf Diesel died?"

"Yes and no."

"Yes and no?"

"We don't know for sure. Probably committed suicide. He had serious financial problems, suffered from bad health, and had become quite depressed. This is why suicide is listed as the cause of death. But the story is very mysterious. After boarding the Dresden for England, Diesel had dinner and retired to his stateroom. He left word to be awakened in the morning. When morning came, Diesel had vanished. His stateroom was empty. Yet his nightshirt had been laid out and his watch placed on the nightstand where he could see it. It seemed he had set everything in order for crawling into bed.

"Ten days later, crewmen aboard a Dutch tugboat found a partially decomposed body floating in the sea. They didn't have room for the body on the little boat so they removed the man's ID, a pocketknife, and an eyeglass case. Diesel's son, Eugen, later identified them as his father's.

"Some don't think it was suicide because the Germans were afraid Diesel would sell his secrets to the English. This would tip the balance in favor of the English. Makes a certain sense, don't you think?"

Tina and Duncan listened wide-eyed to Professor Hooper's story.

"Yes, Carl," Professor Sheets said. "That makes sense. So they returned the body to the sea, and no autopsy was performed?"

"Correct," Professor Hooper said. "That's what they usually did with drowning victims at sea. They committed his body to the deep. So we'll never know for sure what happened to Rudolf

Diesel."

"I think maybe we will," Professor Sheets said, ending the phone call with a brisk key stroke. "I think maybe we will." He sat back in his chair. His eyes went buggy again. "Holy smokes. We may finally have the answer to the mysterious death of Rudolf Diesel." He tossed the phone to Duncan. "Google Rudolf Diesel on the phone and see what he looks like."

Dutifully, Duncan pulled up a picture of the famous German inventor. They compared the image on the screen with the black-and-white photograph from the box. There could be no doubt. Rudolf Diesel met with George Washington Carver in the home of Jenny Jamison. As they all sat there absorbing the implications of what had been discovered, Professor Sheets picked up several handwritten notes.

"Tina," he said. "You said your dad was a chemical engineer. Right?"

"Yes and a very good one."

"Let's copy the notes and formulae from these pages. Would you mind taking them to your dad to see if he can tell us what they mean?"

"I might have to spill the beans," she said.

"No you don't. Tell him you are working on a project for school and found these doodles in a book."

"My dad won't buy that. He's a genius. He'll figure out I'm up to something."

"Well, okay. If he gets too suspicious, let him in on the secret. Do you think he will keep our confidence?"

Tina looked at Professor Sheets with indignation. "Of course he will. My dad is not only a genius, he is an honorable man."

"I'm sure he is, Tina. A most honorable man."

PART TWO

TEN

A Lucky Day

The man stroked his black mustache with a forefinger yellowed by nicotine from two hundred and fifty thousand cigarettes. He lit his first cigarette on his thirteenth birthday. He coughed repeatedly, those deep, raspy smoker's coughs that betray lung damage caused by inhaling decades of toxic crud. Wiping cough tears from his eyes, he peered at the snowy black and white image on his monitor.

"Dorrie, come here," the man said. "Look at this."

The woman heaved herself from a threadbare purple lounge chair, lit her own cigarette, took a long drag, and waddled duck-like over to the desk. The man clicked his mouse and rewound the video to a pre-determined point.

"See them kids at the counter?" he asked.

"Yeah," Dorrie said. "What about it?"

"See that bunny suit they're buying?"

"Yeah. So?"

"Flops over the boy's arm. See that?"

"Did you expect it *not* to flop?" she said, a note of sarcasm in her voice. She took two more deep draws on her cigarette and blew a cloud of smoke.

"Dorrie, come here," the man said. "Look at this."

"Flopping. That's my point. Now look at this," the man said, fast-forwarding the video. "See them walking out of the store. Bunny suit doesn't flop."

"What exactly is your point, Vince?"

"Something's inside the bunny suit. See how stiff it is? There's something in there."

"Yeah. I see it."

"Now look real close at the face opening on the suit. See that dark shadow? I think that's my box."

"But why would them kids steal that box?"

"Dunno. All I know is them kids have crossed a dangerous line. I aim to get that box back, Dorrie. Make no mistake about it."

"Why you so supercharged over that box of old letters?" Dorrie asked. She toddled back to the purple chair and plopped with such a *whoof* that it sent a cloud of dust particles flying into the room.

"What you *don't* know, woman, and what you *need* to know is that them old letters is worth a fortune."

"How so?"

"I checked with that antique document dealer, Ira Badget, the one up in Saint Louis. Told me the set of letters could be worth up to a half a mil if'n they're authentic."

Dorrie's cigarette froze in mid-air. "Half a mil? You didn't tell me that."

"Tellin' you now. Just talked to the guy an hour ago. *Half a mil*, he said. Said he'd come down and look at 'em, give 'em a proper appraisal. That first one, the old one from Carver as a kid? Could be worth ten thou or more, he said. Value is in the whole packet of them. A packet is worth more, he said, than just a single letter. That explain to you why I'm so supercharged?"

"You sure they're authentic?"

"Dorrie, how long I been in the antique business? Huh? How long?"

"Ever since I've knowed you."

"Bingo. And how long is that?"

"Twenty years, I suppose."

"Don't you think in twenty years I'd of learnt how to tell a fake from the real thing?"

"I suppose you *could*, Vince."

"Well, you *could* be right on that count. I know them letters is the real thing. Need to have a certified appraiser like Ira Badget put his say-so on 'em, but I already know the truth of the matter. Sheesh, Dorrie. Sometimes I think you're dumber than them cows you growed up with."

"Meant no offense, Vince."

He shook his head a few times and returned to the monitor. "Got another clue from this security camera too," he said. "Them kids is with a fat guy. Fat guy's into books. Bought an old one a minute or two before them kids scooted out with the bunny suit. Looks to be the boy's old man. Need to find out who that guy is. No doubt he's the one who left me that hundred and twenty smackers." Vince pounded his fist on the desk, rattling an ashtray studded with butts. "That really chaps me off! He knowed how much them letters was worth and he leaves me a lousy hundred and twenty smackers! Like to pop him one. Serve him right."

"Whatcha gonna do, Vince?"

"Dunno. All I know for sure is that I'm gettin' my box back. Don't you doubt it, Dorrie. That box is comin' back to ole Vinny, even if'n I gotta put the hammer down on that fat guy and his chubby spawn. And that little Asian girlie better steer clear. Shouldn'ta messed with ole Vinny. No siree. Shouldn'ta messed with him."

Two days later, Vince put a hand on the inside doorknob of his double-wide trailer and erupted into a coughing spasm lasting the better part of a minute. When he gained control of his lungs, he announced he was heading to the convenience store to buy a carton of Lucky Strikes.

Once behind the wheel of his white Ford van, Vince began to talk to himself. He found talking to himself cleared his thinking and increased his confidence. *First thing... Gotta find out who the fat guy is. Paid in cash. Left no identifying information. Camera in the parking lot not working.* Vince slammed his fist on the steering wheel. *Just my luck! No way to identify the fat guy's vehicle. And them old crows at the cash register. They so busy gabbin' wouldn't notice if the Pope his self walked in and bought twenty-five antique hammers. I tell ya. Not my lucky day. Only clue is the book the fat guy bought. An old book on the westward expansion of these United States. Nobody wants to read an old book on that slop except some history buff. Unfortunately for ole Vinny, they's a lot of old history buffs in these parts. I tell ya. Not my lucky day.*

Vince pulled into the parking lot of the BP gas station and convenience store and lit the last cigarette in the last pack of his last carton. He looked at the glow of the ember on the end of his cigarette and pronounced it *pretty good timing.* Reckoning that he might as well get the full measure of enjoyment, he smoked his cigarette to a stub and continued his musing. *If'n I could just find out who that fat guy is and them whelps, I could track down the box. If'n I knowed where them whelps is goin' to school, could track 'em that way. No way of knowin' though. People come from all over to the antique store. Could be any one of a hundred schools in these parts.* He slammed his fist on the steering wheel again sending tiny cigarette sparks onto his pant legs where they added to the dozens of pinpoint holes already dotting the fabric. *I tell ya. Not my lucky day.*

When he had taken the last pull on his cigarette, Vince pitched the butt through the window and crawled out of his white van. He moseyed into the convenience store and, after another dry, wheezing cough, ordered a carton of Luckies. Behind the counter a young dish-water blond woman ignored Vince while finishing her text message.

"Got a minute!" Vince barked.

"Hold your horses, Gramps," she said. "I heard you. What color Luckies?"

"Silver."

She nodded, reached above her head, slid out a carton of Lucky Strike Silvers, and dropped them on the counter. "Sound of it, you should quit anyway."

"Yeah. And you should lose fifty pounds. Might start with your head. Be a lot better lookin' right away."

"Funny," she said. "That'll be twenty-two forty."

Vince threw a fifty-dollar bill at her. She grabbed it, snapped it twice, and held it up to the light.

"It's genuine," Vince said.

"Lucky for you," she said and counted out the change.

Vince suppressed another cough and started for the door.

Suddenly, he stopped in his tracks and peered at a newspaper on the stand. *Crowder College Welcomes New Faculty Members.* He snatched the paper and held it close to his eyes. "Well I'll be," he said aloud. "Hello fat guy. Hello. Hello. Hello." Vince glanced over his shoulder. "How much for the paper, doll?"

"Dollar ten."

"Here's two bucks. Keep the change. This is Vinny's lucky day after all."

Fifteen minutes later, Vince roared through the entrance to *Heavenly Acres Mobile Home Park* and skidded to a halt in front of his yellow double-wide.

"Hey, Dorrie!" he shouted, bursting through the flimsy front door. "Lucky days are here again!"

Dorrie looked up from her romance novel and squinted over the crooked rims of her black reading glasses. "How's that?"

"Take a gander at this," Vince said, unfurling the paper and pointing a yellowed finger at the photograph of Professor Delbert Sheets.

"So, who's that?" Dorrie asked.

"The fat guy. That's the fat guy on the security video."

"You sure?"

"Course I'm sure. Looks just like him."

"So, if that's the guy, what are ya gonna do?"

"Not sure yet but I'm gonna take a little trip up to Crowder. That's for sure. See what I can stir up."

"I got a bad feeling about this, Vince."

"What's to feel bad about? I got a lead on getting *my* box back. Let's not forget, Dorrie, I bought the box fair and square from that Amish guy. All I'm about to do is get back what is mine."

"Why don't you just call the police?"

"The police. Are you nuts? They'll confiscate the box and who knows if I'll ever get it back. I'm lookin' at half a mil, for crying out loud, Dorrie. Half a mil. We'll blow outta this double-wide and be livin' on Easy Street. Don't you want to live on Easy Street, Dorrie? Sometimes I wonder where your brain is or if you even got one."

"Yeah, I wanna live on Easy Street but I don't wanna live in the state pen. So watch what yer doin' Vince. You got a way of gettin' in trouble."

"Don't you worry your pretty li'l head, Dorrie. I got things under control."

"Right," Dorrie said and returned to her romance novel.

By four-thirty the next afternoon, Vince had drunk a thermos of coffee and chewed his way through twelve chocolate covered cake doughnuts. Cigarette butts clogged the ashtray of his van. Since eight in the morning, he had been sitting in a Crowder College parking lot with his eye on Farber Hall, where the history classes were held. He could see everyone coming and going from Farber Hall but had not laid eyes on Delbert Sheets.

At four-thirty-five, in exasperation, Vince grabbed an antique book he had brought along in case he failed to spot the professor. He stepped out of his van and wandered into Farber Hall. Once inside the building, Vince hunched his shoulders and looked around as if bats would dive bomb him from the ceiling. Having never attended college, Vince displayed considerable uneasiness in these halls of learning.

"May I help you?" the receptionist asked, pulling aside the mouthpiece of her headset.

Vince jumped at the sound of her voice. "Uh, yeah. Lookin' for Mr. Sheets. Delbert Sheets. Got an old history book here. Want to show it to him, maybe give it to him."

"Well, it's *Doctor* Sheets," the receptionist said. "And he's not here today. He is on a recruiting trip to the high schools."

Vince twisted his mouth in frustration. "Well ain't that just peachy! Suppose he'll be back tomorrow?"

"Yes. I will tell him you were here. May I have a name, please?"

"No. No need for that. I'll come back tomorrow." Before the receptionist could say another word, Vince spun on his heals and ran from the building. Back to his van, he cursed under his breath and repeated to himself, *it's never easy, never easy, never easy.*

The following day, Vince resumed his stakeout, this time with better luck. He arrived in time to watch Professor Sheets pop out of his cherry red MINI Cooper, a teeny car for such a big man. Vince remained in place, smoking, eating (Nacho Cheese Doritos this time), and consuming another thermos of coffee. Late in the afternoon, Professor Sheets emerged again from Farber Hall with two students in tow. They stopped to talk for a few minutes before going their separate ways. Professor Sheets stooped to unlock the MINI before tossing his briefcase into the back seat and stuffing himself behind the wheel.

Vince cranked the ignition of his van and whispered to himself, *So,* Doctor *Sheets, a.k.a. fat guy. It's show time. Let's see where you're headed.* He settled in behind Professor Sheets who putt-putted northward out of Neosho. When the traffic thinned, Vince eased back so as not to raise suspicions. He followed his prey into the village of Diamond before turning west on Highway V. Another left on Martin Road took him to the driveway of a rickety old house. Vince slowed his van and crept past the house slow enough to see Duncan and Tina run to greet Professor Sheets. A grin spread across Vince's face as he whispered through clenched teeth, *There's the fat boy and the little Asian girlie babe. Hello fat boy and Asian girlie. So, you go to school in Diamond. Live out in the country. Oh, yes, I believe I've got an idea, a plot is hatching. Yessir, a plot is hatching. Another lucky day for ole Vinny.*

ELEVEN

Art, Science, and Prayer

A sharp three-stroke knock sounded on the front door to the Sheets house on a late Saturday morning in September. Professor Sheets, in his bib overalls and white tee shirt, answered the door, which opened to greet Tina Ng and her father.

"Good morning," Professor Sheets said as he ushered the two visitors into the entry hallway. "Come. Duncan and his mother are finishing breakfast in the kitchen."

When the three entered the kitchen, Mrs. Sheets jumped to her feet, hurried to clear the table, and made room for all to be seated. From his shirt pocket, Marty Ng pulled the sheets of paper upon which Tina had copied the notes and formulae presumably written by George Washington Carver.

"I've looked these notes over," he said. "I find nothing complicated here. The person writing these notes had been developing a process to refine peanut oil for use as a biodiesel fuel. This idea is not new. In fact, Diesel himself used peanut oil in his early work on the engine. Today, several laboratories around the country – particularly at the University of Georgia – are working on peanut oil as a biodiesel fuel. So far, I don't believe they have discovered a process that would make it cost effective for use as a fuel. It holds promise though."

Marty Ng spread the notes on the table. He pointed to one small paragraph on the last page. "This is interesting. This scientist was working to develop a non-edible peanut high in oil. If he succeeded, it would tip the scales in favor of peanut oil as a low-cost fuel alternative."

"Interesting," Professor Sheets said. "Did Tina explain why we asked you to review these notes?"

"She said something about George Washington Carver. I assume he was the author of the notes but she said nothing more. So what gives here?"

"If you agree to keep a secret for a few more months, we will tell you what we have discovered."

"Mum's the word," Marty Ng said.

For the next several minutes, Professor Sheets, with help from Duncan and Tina, recounted the discovery of the box.

"And inside the box we found a wallet with ten thousand dollars in it," Tina said, her brow furrowed in a severe frown. "It's gone. Somebody stole it."

Marty Ng raised his eyebrows. "Ten thousand dollars? Seriously?"

"Seriously," Duncan said. "Tina and I both saw it and she counted the money. When we tracked the box to the Amish work crew and Mr. Beiler, the wallet had disappeared."

Table talk centered for a time on speculations about the disappearance of the wallet. The Beiler boys remained prime suspects as did Dokie Hudspeth, foreman for the Amish carpenters. Since no one knew the chain of possession from the Ng barn to Slick, other wild ideas surfaced. In the end, all agreed the wallet might never be recovered.

"One thing we can now say with confidence," Professor Sheets said, "concerns the true fate of Rudolf Diesel. This letter to George Washington Carver, along with the notes that Mr. Ng has decoded, confirms, in all probability, German agents murdered Diesel. At least new evidence now points in this direction."

"What will you do with this information," Marty asked.

"It is the substance of a paper I hope to publish in a historical journal," Professor Sheets said. "However, I think first we owe it to Rudolf Diesel's family to share the information before going public."

"How will we find his family?" Duncan asked.

Marty Ng raised a hand. "I know a woman named Lucy Lucier who is a private investigator. I shouldn't think it would be too difficult to find out who Diesel's relatives are. Some grandchildren might still be alive though rather old. Surely his great grandchildren would be living. Would you like me to ask Lucy to do this research?"

"How much will it cost?" Professor Sheets asked.

Marty Ng shrugged his shoulders. "She might do it for nothing. If anything, I suspect no more than a hundred dollars."

Professor Sheets nodded. "Let's do it."

"What do you suppose these letters might be worth?" Marty Ng asked as he received a cup of fresh coffee from Mrs. Sheets.

"I have no idea," Professor Sheets said. "There are dealers in rare documents bearing the signatures of famous people. I know some fetch a handsome price."

Fetch a handsome price. Tina looked at Duncan who gave his head a quick shake and rolled his eyes.

"Six, seven figures for the lot of them?" Marty Ng asked.

"I suppose."

"Wow! Then you are sitting on a significant treasure."

"Yes, indeed," Professor Sheets said.

"What do you intend to do with the letters?"

"In due time, we will turn them over to the George Washington Carver National Monument. Before doing so, I want to study them further from a historian's standpoint."

"So you won't sell them?"

"No. That might result in breaking up the body of letters and I think they are best held together. The Monument will know best how to preserve them and make them available for the public. We think that is the best course of action."

"I agree," Marty Ng said. "They are a national treasure."

"Would you like to see them?" Professor Sheets asked.

"Of course," Marty Ng said.

For the next half hour, Professor Sheets displayed the box to Marty Ng. "We take them slowly, one-by-one. It increases the enjoyment and makes our analysis more thorough. I have cataloged all the letters and know, in general, what they contain. However, as an educational project for Tina and Duncan, I have allowed the kids to join me in reading and evaluating the letters. I have one ready to review, shall we have a look?"

All in the Sheets' kitchen nodded with enthusiasm. Out came the clean dishtowel and the freshly laundered cotton gloves. Professor Sheets thumbed through the letters until he came to one dated September 12, 1890.

"Before we look closely at this letter, Duncan and Tina, I think we owe it to Tina's father to let him know what we have learned to date."

For the next several minutes, with the skills of an award-winning teacher, Professor Sheets recounted the contents of the early letters. He explained how George had roamed much of his life in search of education, traveling first to Neosho, then Fort Scott, Olathe, Paola, and Minneapolis, Kansas.

"He wandered away from formal education on several occasions. After Minneapolis, Kansas, he enrolled in a business college where he learned shorthand and typing. He worked for a time at a train station in Kansas City. But..." Professor Sheets raised his professor finger. "He didn't find the job fulfilling. He applied to Highland College in Iowa but something terrible happened. This letter tells a bit of that story. I'll read it. Let's listen."

My dearest Jenny,

At last. I am now enrolled in Simpson College in Winterset, Iowa. As I have written to you before, my quest for a higher education has been a tangled one. I have drifted here and there as a rudderless ship. But now, I am accepted. After the crushing defeat I suffered at Highland College and my wandering as homesteader in Ness County, I am now in great joy. I am taking course work in grammar, mathematics, and etymology. I hope can begin my study of art during the next term.

As a Negro man, I have had my struggles in finding a place to live but, as always, God has provided. The president of Simpson has allowed me to set up my household just off the campus in a small shed. I am doing my laundry business again. Thus far, I have had few customers so my money is very low. I live on beef suet, corn meal, and prayer... often without the suet and meal. Yet, my dear Jenny, I do not despair. God has something very important for me to do. That work demands an education and so the Almighty will provide that education for me. I am involved in Bible study here and the people are so friendly that I finally feel like a real human being.

I yearn to return to Diamond Grove to see you and visit with my Carver folks. I pray that you are well and ask your prayers for me.

With much love and affection,

George

When Professor Sheets finished, he pulled a manila file folder out of his briefcase. "I have my notes on the letters here but I wanted to show you something." Riffling through the pages of handwritten notes, Professor Sheets came to a picture. "Look at this," he said. "I found it online and printed it. Tell me what you see."

Duncan, Tina, Marty, and Mrs. Sheets peered at the picture.

"I see George Washington Carver," Tina said. "He's sitting in the front of a room at an artist's easel."

"Good," Professor Sheets. "What sort of room might this be?"

"It's an art class," Duncan said.

"So it is," Professor Sheets said. "What else do you see?"

"There are one, two, three, four, five women sitting down at easels. That lady there is the teacher," Tina said.

"Excellent," Professor Sheets said. "This is an art class at Simpson College and the teacher is Miss Etta M. Budd. Doctor Carver was an excellent artist and learned some of his technique in Miss Budd's class."

"What happened to him in Highland?" Marty Ng asked.

"Ah," Professor Sheets said. "Good question. It seems he applied to Highland by mail and was accepted. When he arrived on campus, the President took one look at him and refused him entry because he was black."

"That's not fair!" Tina said.

"No, Tina, it isn't. That's the way things were in those days. Even when he was at Simpson College, Miss Etta Budd doubted that a black man could succeed as an artist. George quickly proved her wrong."

"He really believed in God, didn't he Dad?" Duncan said.

"Yes, he did. From my reading, I have discovered that George was a very strong student of the Bible and had a deep prayer life. As he said in the letter, he is convinced that God had an important plan for his life. And he couldn't have been more right. The Christian kindness and charity shown him by the people at Simpson College made him feel human for the first time in his life. That's what's important about church and the community of believers in a church. They help us to feel human."

Marty Ng lowered his gaze to the floor, uncomfortable with the course of this conversation. Tina remained silent, subdued.

An awkward silence followed, which Marty Ng ended by standing and announcing that it was time to leave. He promised to contact Lucy Lucier that day. Professor Sheets walked his visitors to the front door. As they coursed down the hallway, Duncan saw his father put his arm on Marty Ng's shoulder. "How's your daughter Tonya doing?" Duncan couldn't hear the whispered reply but the shake of Marty's lowered head said everything. "We're all praying for her," Professor Sheets said. Marty's head shook again.

An hour later, the Sheets sat around the table savoring the aroma of spaghetti, green beans, and sour dough bread fresh from the oven. They joined hands as Professor Sheets said the blessing in which he emphasized Tonya's struggle in the rehabilitation center. When the prayer had ended and Professor Sheets served the spaghetti, Duncan began to think aloud.

"I wonder why the Ngs don't believe in God."

"Well," Professor Sheets said. "Some people demand proof of God in a scientific way. Marty Ng is a scientist. Maybe that's what he wants to see – scientific proof. And Mrs. Ng immigrated from China. She might have been raised as a Buddhist, if she had any religious upbringing at all. Buddhists don't believe in God. They think God is an invention of human beings because they are afraid of the world around them."

"But Dad. All we have to do is look around us and we can see scientific proof of God. Who else but God could have made galaxies, and mountains, and trees, and butterflies, and… and… and bugs?"

"I agree," Professor Sheets said. "However, many in today's world think somehow the world was created by a giant explosion. That could be true but it begs the question who set off the explosion? Many scientists also believe that millions of years later, some simple elements were combined by accident. Then through an unexplained process, this combination of elements obtained the properties of life, what we might call a life force. This would include the ability to reproduce, metabolize – by this I mean gobble stuff up and gain energy – and evolve into complex life forms."

"But, Dad, that takes as much faith as believing in God."

"I would say more," Mrs. Sheets said. "Now eat your dinner before it gets cold."

"I think it's interesting," Professor Sheets said, mumbling through his chaw of sour dough bread. "George Washington Carver, one of the world's greatest observers of nature, found no problem in crediting it all to God. He saw no contradiction between science and God. In fact, for him, science was a way to understand God more fully."

"Cool," Duncan said. "Really cool."

TWELVE

Preparations

By the second week in October, Vince had completed his plans. For ten consecutive days, he had staked out the Sheets home observing the family's daily patterns. On two separate occasions, he noted the children had taken their bikes to the Carver Monument. He couldn't have been more gleeful. Two kids, riding their bikes on lonely roads with no traffic. Perfect. He could not have designed a more ideal opportunity. Now, all that remained were final details.

Early on a Monday morning, he drove his white van to the Walmart store in Branson. He purchased four cheap prepaid cell phones. *Virtually impossible to track*, Vince said to himself, chuckling under his breath. He bought duct tape, a case of energy bars, a six-pack of water, and three five-gallon gas cans, the red steel kind. He paid cash for everything and, having filled his gas cans, headed back to Blue Eye. Four miles north of town, on Highway 86, he turned onto a dirt road that snaked through a tight cluster of oak trees. He pulled the van into a clearing in front of a pitiful hovel of a house.

He kicked his way through weeds spilling over the walkway leading to a cluttered porch. There, a toothless old woman sat on an upholstered couch picking at the stuffing. Every few seconds, she took a sip of amber liquid from a glass encrusted with who-knows-what.

"Mornin', Lena," Vince said. "Large Lewis around?"

"Gone to the store, be home shortly. Want to set a spell an' wait?"

"Sure," Vince said plopping on the torn cusion."

Lena lifted her glass. "Whiskey?"

"No thanks, Lena. Don't drink anymore. Twenty years sober now."

"Shame," Lena said, taking a swig. "Yer feelin' the best yer gonna feel all day. For me the best is yet to come."

"If you say so."

"How's the antique business? You still managing that place? Whatcha call it?"

"Dead People's Rejects," Vince said. "Yup, still managing the place. Business is good. Owner is in Little Rock. Never comes by. No micromanaging."

"No micro- what?"

"Never mind."

Vince and Lena sat in silence for fifteen long minutes before a beat-up blue Ford pickup emerged from the tree canopy into the clearing. A giant of a man ballooned out of the cab carrying a plastic sack with two bottles of cheap whiskey. Vince watched him as he trampled the weeds under his feet *en route* to the porch.

The man's vacant pale-blue eyes and slack jaw betrayed his mental incompetence. Lena once told Vince that Large Lewis functioned at a fourth-grade level. He could read and write simple sentences but even the most elementary arithmetic extended beyond his reach. The multiplication tables were mystifying and long division completely baffled him. Vince wondered how the man ever passed the test to obtain a driver's license. Yet, Large Lewis not only drove legally, he found work, mostly odd jobs. He moved furniture, cleaned grease traps, did seasonal logging work, and performed any other form of employment that involved considerable brawn but little brain. And that was precisely why Vince had come in search of Large Lewis on this particular Monday morning.

"Oh hi, Vince," Large Lewis said in a slow drawl. "Why you

here?"

"Need to have you help me with a project."

"Doin' what?"

"Need to speak in private. Why don't you give your ma them bottles and join me out by the van?"

Lena accepted the plastic sack without saying a word. Vince guided Large Lewis to the far side of the van. Before he could present his job offer, Vince collapsed in a long coughing spasm. Large Lewis, in an effort to help, whacked Vince on the back with such strength that it drove the black-haired man to one knee. When the cough abated, Vince hauled himself to an unsteady stance. He snagged another cigarette and lit it behind cupped hands.

"Some kids stole something of mine, Lewis," Vince said blowing out a stream of smoke. "Need your help getting it back."

"Okay, what I gotta do?"

"These kids got a valuable box of mine. Stole it right outta my office. Took it to their home. What I got in mind is to steal one of the kids until his folks cough up the box. I need you to help me get the kid. Tit-for-tat, as they say. Eye-for-an-eye. You steal from me, I steal from you."

"Dunno, Vince. Don't sound right. Be kidnappin' won't it?"

"Nah. Not when yer just tryin' to get back somethin' what belongs to you in the first place. They'll give up the box in a flash. Then the kid goes back to the parents. No harm, no foul. You follow?"

"I reckon. How much?"

"How's five hundred sound?"

Large Lewis raised his upper lip in a moronic smile. "Oh that do sound good, Vince. When?"

"Not sure. Gotta wait for the kids to ride their bikes along this one road up by Neosho. We'll hang out for a few days 'til we spot 'em on the road. They ride on this road every few days after school. So we'll go up there startin' tomorrow and just wait 'til we see 'em. When we do, we'll drive beside 'em. You'll reach out the van door and nab the boy. Let the girl go. Boy's the one that took the box."

"Then what?"

"Then you're done. I drop you off and pay you five hundred smackers."

Large Lewis took two minutes to process this offer in his feeble mind before offering a slow nod. "Okay."

"Deal?" Vince asked.

"Deal," Large Lewis said.

"Okay, now listen close. Tomorrow you meet me at one o'clock in the parking lot of the outlet mall in Branson. Tomorrow. One o'clock. Outlet mall. Branson. Got it?"

Large Lewis smiled around his blackened tooth snags. "Got it boss."

"Good. See you tomorrow."

The men shook hands, which Vince regretted. Rubbing his crushed knuckles, and suffering another coughing jag, Vince climbed into the white van and drove home to the yellow double-wide trailer.

Later that evening, he drove back to Branson to the Clay Cooper Theater where Branson's most popular show – the Haygoods – played to a full house. Once dark had descended upon the tourist town, Vince slipped from his white van and ducked behind a row of cars in a far corner of the parking lot. A line of trees provided added obscurity in the moonless night. He studied the license plate mountings of several cars before exchanging his own van plates with those of an inconspicuous white Ford Taurus. He also retrieved a set of plates he had stolen several days earlier in the long-term lot of the Branson Airport. These he placed on yet another car and chucked the plates from that car into his van. This provided him with one set of stolen plates in reserve. *Most people don't look at their plates, especially at night,* he reasoned to himself. *Besides, when they discover the switch, they will be mightily confused, as will the stupid cops. Take 'em a day to figure it out. By then I'll be long gone.*

The next afternoon, Vince picked up Large Lewis and drove him to Burger King where he ordered four Whoppers and a giant Coke. The big man's appetite knew no bounds. While Large Lewis stuffed the hamburgers in his mouth, Vince began the two-hour drive to Diamond, Missouri. Once there, they pulled off onto a wide spot of Elder Road, obscured by giant oak trees. There they waited, watching for any sign of Duncan or Tina. By six o'clock in the evening, they realized there would be no sightings of the children, so they made their way back to Blue Eye.

The same outcome befell them on Wednesday, Thursday, and the following Monday. On Tuesday, as Vince cranked the ignition for yet another empty-handed drive to Blue Eye, he spotted two figures in his rear view mirror. Two kids on bikes.

"Lewis! Wake up! I see 'em."

Large Lewis opened one ignorant eye and tried to remember where he was and why. As he regained awareness of his circumstances, he raised his seat, which compressed his stomach and forced a loud, smelly belch.

"Get ready, Lewis," Vince said, revving his engine. "As soon as they pass, I'll ease alongside them. The boy's in the back. He's our target. When I'm right next to him, you reach out and grab him, pull him into the van. Got it?"

"Got it, boss."

With surprising speed and dexterity, Large Lewis turned in his seat and stepped into the back of the van. He opened the sliding side door and crouched… waiting.

Thirteen

Elder Road

Pig-tailed twin girls and their parents paused by the orange lounge chairs in the lobby of the Monument. There Gideon shared new information with Duncan and Tina.

"You see," Gideon was saying. "At Simpson College George made a dramatic change in his plans. For a long time, he thought he would be an artist and, as you can tell from his artwork in this museum, he was a good artist. However, Etta Budd, his art teacher, introduced George to her father who taught horticulture at Iowa Agricultural College and Model Farm. We now know this institution as Iowa State University. Professor Budd urged Doctor Carver to study agriculture because it would provide a greater opportunity for service to the African American race."

"Did he give up art after that?" Duncan asked.

"Absolutely not," Gideon said. "He continued to paint and one of his paintings, *Yucca and Cactus*, won an honorable mention award at the World's Fair in 1893."

For a long time, he thought he would be an artist.

"But he liked Iowa Agricultural College?" Tina asked.

"Not at first. He suffered racial insults and had difficulty finding a place to live. Finally, the head of the Agricultural Experiment Station allowed him to live in one of the empty offices on campus. The man who ran the dining hall on campus made Doctor Carver eat his meals in the basement with the food service workers. He couldn't eat with the other students because he was black."

The two little girls who had stopped to listen became so interested they sat on the floor, cross-legged, to hear more. "That wasn't nice," one of them said.

"No, it was not," Gideon continued. "But something wonderful happened. George wrote to a friend of his, a white friend who had once been his painting partner. Her name was Sophia Liston. In his letter, George told what had happened in the dining hall. Do you know what Sophia Liston did?"

The children shook their heads in unison.

"Well," Gideon said, his eyes twinkling. "She put on her best dress and hat, jumped on the train, and traveled to Ames Iowa. When she arrived on campus, she joined George and ate with him in the basement of the dining hall. Then she paraded around campus arm-in-arm with him in a show of support for her friend. That did it. After that, George made many friends, ate with the other students, and over time became quite popular."

"Still it must have been hard," the blond girls' mother said.

"Yes, I'm sure it was, but George Washington Carver relied on his faith. When he was confronted with such racism, he no doubt recited his favorite passage from the Bible, Proverbs 3:6. *In all thy ways acknowledge Him, and He shall direct thy paths.*"

The conversation about George's meals in the basement prompted Duncan to pull the family cell phone from his pocket. "Holy cow!" he said. "It's nearly five o'clock. We better get started for home, Tina. If I'm late for dinner, I'll be in big trouble."

Tina nodded and the two of them thanked Gideon as they raced out of the building to the bike rack. Tina pumped hard to gain the lead, which was fine with Duncan who had no interest in racing. By the time they turned on Elder Road heading west, Tina was a good fifty yards ahead and passed the driveway to the Jones farm several seconds before Duncan. He fought the sun in his eyes and didn't see a white van emerging from the copse of trees to his right. As the van drew near, he turned his bike to the edge of the asphalt and steered carefully so as not to slide into the ditch.

The white van nosed by him.

The white van nosed by him. Focused on keeping his balance, Duncan did not see the side door of the van slide open. A steel arm coiled around him, jerked him from his bike, and threw him against the far wall of the van.

"Bind him up with that duct tape," ordered the driver as he punched the accelerator and shot past Tina.

Large Lewis pinned Duncan to the floor of the van, snatched his hands behind his back, and wound several tight loops of duct tape around his wrist and ankles. A six-inch strip of duct tape stitched his mouth to silence. Large Lewis returned to the passenger seat, leaving Duncan to roll from side-to-side in the van as it careened around curves at breakneck speed.

Kidnapped! When the reality hit Duncan, his stomach tightened in a knot of black dread. *What do these guys want with me? Where are they taking me? Are they going to hurt me? Are they going to kill me? Did Tina see the van? Maybe she got the license plate? How can I get this tape off?* These thoughts looped through his mind as he crashed into a pile of mover's pads reeking of musty filth.

The two men said nothing, which intensified Duncan's terror. He had no clue why he had been taken prisoner nor could he ask questions from behind the duct tape gag. *Why me? My mom and dad don't have money. Not enough to make it worthwhile to kidnap me. Will I ever see my parents again? Oh please, God, don't let them hurt me. Don't let them kill me.*

As the sun descended below the horizon, Duncan cleared his head. He put his mind to ways he might escape or lead others to him. Just then, it occurred to him that his family cell phone was in the pocket of his jeans. *I remember my dad saying the cell phone has a GPS device. Maybe they can track me. If I can get my hands free, I can get to the phone. Does it have to be turned on to be tracked? Or can they track it anyway? Don't know. I'll try to punch it on just to be sure. In all thy ways acknowledge Him, and He shall direct thy paths.* These thoughts played to the steady thrum of tires on blacktop.

~~~

"Watch it buddy!" Tina screamed as the white van shot past her causing her to veer off the road into the ditch. She pitched off her bike and skidded along the ground, scraping her knee. She shook her fist at the retreating van. "Dumb jerk!" She sat on the ground, wincing at the pain in her knee. She tried to daub the blood with a tissue pulled from the pocket of her cherry red shorts.

Glancing behind, all she could see were the last spins of Duncan's front wheel. Thinking he may have run into the stand of trees, Tina cried, "Duncan! Duncan! Duncan Sheets! Not funny. I need some help here." When he did not appear, Tina stood and limped toward his bike. She stood over it, hands on her narrow hips and surveyed her surroundings. Nothing. She made her way into the stand of trees, figuring Duncan was peeing. "Couldn't you have waited until we got home?" Again, nothing.

A worm of worry wriggled around in her mind. "Duncan?" she called again. Still no answer. Back on the road, she spun in a slow three-hundred-and-sixty degree scan. Seeing nothing, she raked through the roadside weeds fearing that the white van had run over Duncan. Would she find his crushed and lifeless body sprawled in the jungle of wild plants growing along the ditch? Finding nothing, Tina limped to her bike as fast as her wounded knee would permit.

It took another ten minutes for her to reach the front yard of the Sheets house where she jumped off her bike and ran into the house without knocking. Professor Sheets sat reading his paper and Mrs. Sheets was peering into the open oven when Tina burst into the kitchen screaming, "I can't find him! Duncan! He's gone!"

FOURTEEN

Dread

"What? What are you saying, dear?" Mrs. Sheets said, rising from the oven.

Tina recounted what had happened, her words spewing like water from an open hydrant.

"Slow down, honey, I can't understand what you are saying," Mrs. Sheets said.

Tina repeated herself, slower this time. Professor and Mrs. Sheets looked at one another, worry etched on their faces. Professor Sheets dropped his paper on the table and stood. "Come," he said. "Show us."

They ran to the Sheets' minivan, and buckled their seatbelts. While Professor Sheets pulled out of the driveway, Mrs. Sheets checked her cell phone for a text or voice mail message from Duncan. Nothing. She called his number three times. No answer. "Phone must be switched off," she said, placing her hand over her mouth and staring out the window. Professor Sheets said nothing. They parked by the bike, jumped from the minivan, and called Duncan's name in all directions.

Graveyard silence.

Professor Sheets picked up his son's bike and put it into the back of the minivan.

"Let's go down to that house. I think their name is Jones. Maybe they've seen him," he said, his voice subdued.

As they pulled into the lane leading to the Jones' house, Mrs. Sheets spotted Mr. Jones on the side patio firing up his grill.

"Evening," Professor Sheets said.

Mister Jones nodded and walked toward the minivan. They shook hands.

"Looking for my son. He was riding down this road a few minutes ago and has suddenly disappeared. Twelve-year-old boy. Have you seen him?"

"No, sir," Mr. Jones said. "Just came out of the house though. What happened?"

Professor Sheets repeated what he had heard from Tina.

Mister Jones shook his head. "I'll keep an eye out for him. Let me get your number."

"The van," Tina piped. "What about a white van? Did you see a white van?"

"Come to think of it," Mr. Jones said. "For the past few days I have seen a white van driving up and down Elder Road. Once I saw it parked in a stand of trees up the road a ways. Never thought much of it at the time."

The Sheets thanked Mr. Jones and headed back to the house.

"We better call the police," Mrs. Sheets said, fighting tears.

"Yes," was all Professor Sheets said.

Within five minutes of the fateful phone call, two Diamond police cruisers rolled into the Sheets' driveway. The police chief, Biggie Tipton, a tiny man of no more than one hundred forty pounds bounded from his car up the front steps of the porch. Behind him ran Sergeant Patsy O'Keefe, the second of three officers employed by the town of Diamond. Both Chief Biggie Tipton and Sergeant Patsy O'Keefe were well trained and competent. They could have found employment in a much larger police department but both had family ties in the region. Biggie's wife was the Superintendent of Schools and Patsy's husband ran a sizeable angus ranch to the east of town. The mayor of Diamond counted himself fortunate to have two officers of such skill and intelligence.

In the Sheets' front room, Biggie and Patsy listened to Tina as she again recounted the circumstances surrounding Duncan's disappearance. They asked several clarifying questions and took copious notes. When they had finished the interview, Chief Tipton asked Tina to lead them to the alleged crime scene. The officers examined the area where the van had hidden. There were seventy-six Lucky Strike Silver butts strewn in the underbrush. With latex gloved hands Sergeant O'Keefe placed several of the cigarette butts in a plastic baggie.

"Well, one thing is for sure," Chief Biggie Tipton said. "Whoever did this is stupid. His – or her, or their – DNA will be smeared all over these cigarette butts. That will no doubt help us down the road. We better get this area secured and process the scene as soon as possible."

"I'll reach out to County and some neighboring departments for help," Sergeant Patsy O'Keefe said.

"Better call the State office too," Chief Tipton said. "And the FBI. They can help with their Evidence Response Team Unit."

Ten minutes later, a state highway patrol car arrived on the scene.

"What have we got here?" Lieutenant Orrin Onofrio asked, putting on his Smoky Bear hat.

Using law enforcement lingo such as *non-family abduction, critical incident, perps,* and *investigative scene*, Chief Tipton and Sergeant O'Keefe described the apparent abduction. For several minutes, the officers discussed the next procedures to follow while Tina and the Sheets stood by, frantic with worry.

Lieutenant Onofrio walked over to where the three were standing. "We believe this is likely an abduction and meets the legal criteria for issuing an Amber Alert. We will need to get a complete description of Duncan, including what he was wearing. Mister and Mrs. Sheets, I'll come back to the house with you to collect that information. We will also need to get a recent picture of your son.

"You said your son carries a cell phone. We will do what we can to track that phone. We can get authorization for what we call an *emergency ping* to help locate the cell phone. This could prove to be our best shot at locating the van. However, the carrier you used in Florida is much weaker here with fewer cell towers. So tracking may be difficult, especially if they headed south where the terrain is much hillier with deep draws and hollows. Please be assured, we will be persistent in our efforts.

"Now, let's return to the house. Sergeant O'Keefe will take Tina home and visit with her parents. Lieutenant Onofrio will await the other officers. We will begin a neighborhood canvas to see if anyone has spotted the van or seen anything suspicious. We might even get lucky and get some security camera footage, though that is unlikely."

Unable to withhold her emotion, Mrs. Sheets coughed and uttered a long, unnatural moan into the evening sky. She burst into uncontrolled sobbing, clinging to her husband. With his arm encircling his wife, Professor Sheets stared into the evening sky. He bore such a vacant look that one might have thought him a standing corpse.

"We will work quickly," Chief Tipton said. "The first twenty-four to forty-eight hours can be critical."

An hour later, the Amber Alert had been issued. Every law-enforcement agency in southern Missouri, northern Arkansas, and eastern Oklahoma were notified of the potential abduction. Roadblocks were erected on the major highways. However, the multitude of secondary and side roads in the region proved to be a major problem for law enforcement. Criminals could find unblocked routes.

The Amber Alert sounded on Mrs. Sheets' cell phone and those awful white letters against an ink black screen recorded the abduction of her son. "Dear God, please…" was all she could say.

~~~

Simultaneously, the Amber Alert sounded on Vince's cell phone and the one wedged into Duncan's front pocket. Vince jerked the phone from his shirt pocket and read the alert. "Already! They're on it already!" He slammed the palm of his hand against the steering wheel and broke out in a coughing spell. In wheezing bursts of speech, he ordered Large Lewis to crawl into the back of the van, get Duncan's cell phone, and *smash it to smithereens.*

To Duncan's wide-eyed horror, Large Lewis climbed into the back of the van, pawed around Duncan's pockets until he found the cell phone. He placed the phone on the floorboard and, with boots the size of tugboats, stomped it into a pile of electronic debris.

"Good job," Vince said. "That solves that problem. Shoulda checked for a cell phone when we nabbed him. They're after the van though. Gotta ditch it. We're gonna pull into a parking lot somewhere in Monett and hot wire a car. Gotta find a secluded parking lot after dark. Ditch the van there, put them spare plates on the new car, and head back to Branson. Then you're on your way, five hundred smackers richer."

"Oh that's good, boss. Can we get somethin' to eat in Monett? I'm starving'."

"No chance. No time to eat. You can get something after we part ways in Branson."

Vince shook a Lucky Strike Silver from its pack and smoked with nervous haste. Recognizing that he would have better luck on back roads, Vince turned from Highway 86 onto Missouri Highway EE toward the Capps Creek Recreation Area. Once in the state park, he eased behind a service building, and killed the engine. Taking the last drag on his cigarette, he told Large Lewis they would wait there until dusk faded to dark. "Keep yer fingers crossed, Lewis, that no one spots us here. Some of these folks probably got that cussed Amber Alert."

Lewis displayed his crossed fore and index fingers. "Yes, boss. Got 'em crossed," he said on a wave of bad breath.

As dark descended upon the conservation area, Duncan listened to the slamming of car doors and sounds of departure from the state park. He shoved his lingering dread to the back of his mind. It hovered there, menacing, but he possessed a renewed clarity of mind that panic had until now squelched. He scoured his brain for ideas that could direct his escape but no practical, workable notions came to mind.

"Figure we can go now, boss?" Large Lewis said. "I starvin'."

"Soon. Want to be among the last ones to leave. Don't want ever'one remembering us pulling out of the park. Follow?"

"No. Not for sure," Lewis said, his fingers still crossed.

"Well, don't worry about it."

Five minutes slid by in silence before Vince fired the van engine. In an English accent, a female voice from Vince's phone directed them from the park onto a series of backcountry roads leading to Monett. Twenty minutes later, they slipped into the parking lot of Monett's Walmart Supercenter.

"See them string of cars on the far edge of the lot?" Vince said.

"I see 'em, boss."

"Employees, I figure. Most shoppers want to park close to the store. Management would make employees park far out from the doors to let customers have the closer parking spots. Follow?"

"I think so."

"Point is, them cars is not likely to be approached 'til the end of the shift. We gotta hope that ain't too soon." Vince scanned the row of thirteen cars. "Gold Toyota Highlander. That'll have to do. Popular car. Popular color. Wait here." He grabbed a tool from the back known as a slim jim, a screwdriver, and the stolen license plates. Ten minutes later, he knocked on Large Lewis' window. "Let's go," he said. "Bring the kid. I'll get the gas cans, water, and power bars."

Large Lewis reached in from the side door of the van, grabbed Duncan, and slung him over his shoulder like a sack of potting soil.

"Throw him in the back seat." Vince threw Duncan a menacing look. "And not a peep from you, kid, understand?" Duncan nodded. "Okay, Lewis, we're ready to go. You follow me in the van."

"Where we goin' boss?"

"We'll drive the van away from here to divert the cops' attention from the carjacking. We'll ditch the van out in the country somewhere. Then you'll hop in this Highlander for the trip to Branson. Ready?"

"I think so, boss."

"Good, let me get my gun before we take off."

Gun!

At that moment, a new wave of dread washed over Duncan as he realized the *boss* and Lewis had made no effort to disguise themselves. If he got out alive, he could identify the two men and help put them away. A gun. No, they had no intention of keeping him alive. None at all.

FIFTEEN

Vigil

Throughout the evening, Chief Tipton and Sergeant O'Keefe continued to question the Sheets in an effort to develop further leads. Having determined the Sheets were not people of great wealth, the probability of kidnapping for ransom seemed remote. A kidnapping for more sadistic purposes lurked as the unspoken horror.

"It's a few minutes before ten o'clock. Not much more we can do but wait," Chief Biggie Tipton said. "We've contacted the FBI agent in Joplin. He is returning from a training program in Quantico, Virginia. I've briefed him and he will join us as soon as he gets back to town. The Evidence Response Team from Saint Louis is on its way. So, I'll soon be on my way. We do not know if, when, or how you may be contacted by the perps. However, should either of your cell phones ring and you do not recognize the number or the caller, do *not* answer the phone. Let the attending officer take the call. We will have someone with you around the clock until it is no longer necessary. Clear?"

The Sheets nodded and thanked the police chief for waiting with them for five hours hoping for an early break. Given the hour, Chief Tipton figured nothing would happen until the next day, at the earliest. The Ngs had also joined them in the front room of the Sheets' home for a few hours to give support but had already left. Professor and Mrs. Sheets remained to endure the longest and most agonizing night of their lives.

Mrs. Sheets sat on the edge of their bed, her eyes puffy from crying, her nose swollen from a hundred tissue wipes. Professor Sheets' stood by her side. His mouth drooped at the corners and his once proud mustache hung limp and unraveled. He whispered a short prayer.

The night passed in agonizing slowness. Professor and Mrs. Sheets tossed and turned, wadding the sheets, twisting their pajamas, and slamming the pillows with head and hand. Having just glimpsed 5:46 on the digital alarm clock, Professor Sheets rolled over to hug his wife when suddenly he shot upright in bed. Mrs. Sheets cast a bleary eye in his direction.

"You don't suppose," Professor Sheets asked his wife.

"Suppose what?"

"The box! Do you suppose whoever took Duncan was after the box?"

"Who would take our boy for an antique box, Delbert? That makes no sense."

"Still, I'm going to mention it to the police."

In a tattered green terrycloth robe and scuffed slippers, Professor Sheets lumped down the stairs just as Sergeant Patsy O'Keefe pulled up.

"How are you folks holding up?" she asked, lowering herself to the green couch.

"Didn't get much sleep. Spent the night praying," Professor Sheets said.

"So did I," Sergeant O'Keefe said. "You know, last night we assumed if this is a kidnapping for ransom, there would be money involved. What we didn't establish is whether there could be something else of value: jewelry, stocks, real estate, anything like that."

"Funny thing you should ask. Just a few minutes ago, I thought something."

"Please, tell me."

"It's a box. A box of historic letters, a jackknife, two old photographs of this house, and three rocks."

Sergeant O'Keefe's brow furrowed. "And why is this worth money?"

"I'm not sure it is, but here is the story…"

For the next several minutes, Professor Sheets recounted the discovery of the box by Duncan and Tina. He explained the chain of possession, his own "re-purchasing" of the box, and the research on its contents. When he finished, he looked at Sergeant O'Keefe. "I suppose I'm in trouble over buying back the box."

Sergeant O'Keefe raised her eyebrows and pursed her lips. After several long seconds, she said, "We will not worry about that. So you think the letters from George Washington Carver might be worth a good deal of money?"

"I'm not sure. I've not had them appraised but they could be."

"Do you believe it's possible that this black-haired, black-mustached antique dealer could have kidnapped your son to get the box back?"

Professor Sheets shrugged. "I have no idea. Never met the man, but I can think of no other possibility. Who else would want to kidnap Duncan?"

Sergeant O'Keefe closed her notebook. "I'll call in this information and have the Highway Patrol check into the antique dealer. What was the name of the store?"

"Dead People's Rejects."

Sergeant O'Keefe shook her head. "Cute," she said with unveiled sarcasm.

Professor Sheets nodded.

Shortly after eleven o'clock the Ngs returned with a Chinese pork casserole and a bowl of mixed fruit. They joined the Sheets in a silent vigil, waiting for the dreaded call. As noon approached, they heard another knock on the door. When Professor Sheets opened the door, he beheld a distinguished gray-haired man in a black clergy shirt with white tab collar.

"Good morning," the clergyman said. "I'm Gideon Graham."

"Ah, Gideon… I mean Reverend Graham, please come in."

"Gideon is fine. I received the Amber Alert on my cell phone last night. I thought I should come by and, if nothing else, pray with you for Duncan's safe return."

"That's very good of you," Professor Sheets said. "Duncan so enjoys his time with you and so does Tina. She is here right now with her parents."

When Gideon entered the front room, Tina put her arms around his waist in a tight hug. Gideon patted her back until she broke away and returned to her parents' side. From experience, Gideon knew that retelling the events of a crisis often eases tension. Once seated, he asked, "What happened?"

Tina immediately explained what had taken place after she and Duncan left the Monument. Gideon fixed his eyes on all in the room. "We have a large prayer chain," he said. "I will be sure and put you folks on it as soon as I leave. You will have legions of people praying for Duncan's safe return. And now, I would like to pray with you."

The Ngs stood in unison. "We should be going. We'll leave you to the prayer."

"Please don't go," Gideon said. "Your prayers are needed too."

"But we aren't believers," Marty Ng said.

"Jesus said, 'whoever comes to me, I will not cast out.' God can answer the unselfish prayers of those who do not yet believe. So, please, sit down and join us. I know we would all appreciate it."

Mrs. Ng looked at her shoes, Tina crossed her arms over her chest, and Marty looked intently at Gideon. The Ng family then lowered to the couch and bowed their heads. Sergeant O'Keefe clasped her hands and closed her eyes.

Gideon implored God to foil the perpetrators and return Duncan to his parents, alive and well. He prayed for the officers working on the case and for a new level of patience and faith. When he finished, he took his leave, promising to return later in the day after his shift at the Monument. The Ngs said nothing but accepted the invitation to stay for the Chinese pork casserole and fruit medley.

~~~

The afternoon wore on. The Sheets were alone again, except for Sergeant O'Keefe, when at four o'clock they heard a tentative knock on the door. Professor Sheets answered the door to a somber Isaac Beiler and an attractive woman in a long blue dress. She wore a small white cap on her head. Isaac Beiler carried a wicker basket covered with white muslin. In the distance, washed in light from the porch lamp, Dokie Hudspeth leaned against his truck picking his teeth with a strand of straw.

"Mister Beiler," Professor Sheets said. "Please come in. I presume this is Mrs. Beiler?"

"My wife, Hannah," Isaac Beiler said. "We heard about your son. We brought you food – fried chicken, sauerkraut, Amish bread, and apple pie."

"How did you hear about Duncan?"

"Mister Hudspeth heard the Amber Alert and came to our farm. We wanted to help. Mr. Hudspeth offered to drive us here."

"Very kind of you. Let me introduce you to my wife," Professor Sheets said. He called Dokie Hudspeth to join them. The foreman waived them off, saying he would wait by his truck. Professor Sheets tried to persuade him otherwise but Dokie declined and said he was waiting for a call on an upcoming job.

Sergeant O'Keefe excused herself to join Hudspeth. "I have a few questions for him," she said, whispering over her shoulder.

Hannah Beiler took one look at the disheveled Linda Sheets and put her arms around the poor woman and murmured, "The Old Amish are praying for thee." Mrs. Sheets nodded and sniffed before wiping her raw nose. The four sat in the living room. The two women talked about food and recipes. Professor Sheets and Isaac Beiler remained silent, staring at their shoes.

Another knock sounded on the front door. Chief Biggie Tipton strode into the room and announced the white van had been located. "We found it parked on a side road southeast of Monett. The license plates have been changed, but we ran the vehicle identification number. It is registered to Vincent Puglisi, the manager of Dead People's Rejects in Blue Eye. The ashtray was stuffed with Lucky Strike Silver butts. So, we have him, or them, on the run. Unfortunately, we found the smashed remains of the cell phone your son was carrying. No possibility of phone tracking now. We are all over the antique store and Puglisi's home like white on rice. So far, we haven't sighted him… or them. We figure Puglisi's wife is with him. We will put their pictures and descriptions out to all law enforcement agencies."

Professor Sheets hung his head, overcome by the news of the crushed cell phone. After a long silence, he raised it. "Do we have any idea where they are or what they are driving?"

"None, I'm sorry to say, but don't give up hope. This is a

positive development. So keep the faith."

With that, Chief Tipton tipped his hat and departed. Sergeant O'Keefe also took her leave as an officer with the Neosho Police Department came on duty for the evening and night hours.

Sixteen

Twisted Cedar Gap

Vince eased the Toyota Highlander next to Large Lewis' blue pickup. The outlet mall was nearly deserted by the time they arrived and Vince hurried to dispatch Large Lewis. He palmed a wad of money, folded and wrapped in a broccoli band. Peeling five one hundred dollar bills from the wad, he said, "There you go. Five hundred smackers. Remember, mum is the word. You don't know nothin'. Get it?"

"Got it boss."

Vince shoved the money into Lewis' shirt pocket and gave it a little pat. He wasted no time racing from the parking lot and on to the crowded streets of a tourist night in Branson. Duncan lay in the back seat, his mind whirring. He had begun to piece together bits of significant information. *I saw two neon signs that said Branson. We're in Branson for sure. Boss has slicked back black hair and black mustache. A Hawaiian shirt. Is the boss Slick? Is this about George Washington Carver's box? Will the boss hold me in ransom for the return of the box? Maybe. The letters must be worth a lot. Won't he keep me alive to get the box? Then what? The black gun. I see the black gun right there in the console box. O Lord, then what?*

After twenty minutes of stop-and-go traffic, Vince hit the accelerator and settled the Toyota into a high-speed run. From where he lay, Duncan could see a digital compass on the rearview mirror. They were headed south. Fifteen minutes later, Vince turned west and lowered his speed to negotiate a curvy road. *Must be heading to Blue Eye. Seems like the same route we took with my dad. Yes, it's Slick, for sure. He wants the box.*

Another twenty minutes passed before Vince slowed the Toyota and skidded to a stop. He slid the gun under his belted trouser tops and retrieved a jackknife from his hip pocket. He opened the back door to the van, slit the duct tape binding Duncan's ankles, and jerked him to a sitting position. "Get out and walk slowly into the yellow house," he said, brandishing his gun.

Inside the double-wide, a billowy woman with stringy, black-rooted blond hair stood from her purple chair and stared, mouth agape.

"Vincent! What you done?"

"No time to jaw, woman. Get a suitcase out and pack us up for several days. We gotta move. Cops are on our trail."

"Move? Cops? I ain't doin' nothin' Vince 'til you tell me what's goin' on."

"Figure it out, Dorrie. How dumb can you be? This is the fat guy's kid. We're fixin' to set up a swap. The box for the kid."

"Vince, you moron! This is kidnapping! The cops will be all over this like ticks on a pup. Feds will come after us."

"How do you know?"

"I know 'cause I read it once in one of my stories. Feds come in when they's a kidnappin'. What you thinkin'?"

"Just get the suitcase ready. Gotta move."

Vince and Dorrie stared rigidly at one another for a good ten seconds before Dorrie melted and waddled into the bedroom muttering under her breath. "This better work Vince or Easy Street is gonna be in the joint."

When she disappeared, Duncan uttered *mmph* sounds from behind the duct tape. Vince jerked the tape from Duncan's mouth. Tears welled in Duncan's eyes.

"Whaddya want?" Vince asked.

"I have to pee," Duncan said.

"Bathroom's in there," Vince said gesturing with his pistol.

"I need my hands free."

Vince looked stupidly at Duncan for several seconds before realizing that it would be difficult for the boy to relieve himself with bound hands. He slit the duct tape on Duncan's wrists. "Make it fast."

The bathroom reeked of cigarette smoke and something sour. He lifted the chipped wood toilet seat and peered into a moldy bowl. When he finished, Duncan tried to get his hands clean with a bar of rough soap and water splashing into an encrusted sink. He dried his hands on his jeans avoiding the grime-caked green hand towel hanging askew on the rack.

Vince wasted no time in binding Duncan's hands once more. To the relief of Duncan's burning mouth, Vince did not replace the gag.

"No gag. No tapin' your feet. But no funny business, hear? Now sit down and don't move." Vince waggled the gun.

Ten minutes later, the billowy woman returned carrying a large hard-sided suitcase, a brown old timer such as Duncan had seen in antique stores. "Where we goin' Vince?"

"They's an old rich crow named Elvira Applegate. She come to the store the other day. Blabbed all around that her and her old man were leavin' the next day for a tour of the Greek Isles. Be gone a month."

"Yeah. So?"

"She got a place down just above the Arkansas line. In them hills by Twisted Cedar Gap. Secluded. Can't hardly find it if'n you don't know where to look. I know where the key is hid 'cause I delivered a piece of antique furniture to her a few months back. They's a key hidden in a fake rock in the rock garden by the back door. Key's probably still there. So let's get to crackin'. Get up kid."

Duncan led the two of them out to the Highlander and resumed his position, lying on the back seat. Dorrie threw the suitcase into the rear of the car and heaved herself into the passenger seat. As soon as the car doors closed, both Vince and Dorrie lit cigarettes. Duncan felt a measure of relief that he hadn't inherited his father's asthma.

Vince turned the key.

The engine jumped to life.

They peeled gravel.
Next stop – Twisted Cedar Gap.
Then what?

SEVENTEEN

A Grate

Duncan remained vigilant. Despite being bound, he continued to search for a means of escape. He figured if he could get away from Vince and Dorrie, and neither had the gun, he could outrun them both. Vince couldn't go over five steps without collapsing in a coughing fit and Dorrie had more blubber than an elephant seal. Even at his top speed of *slow*, Duncan would leave them in his dust. However, with his hands taped together behind his back, he had limited options. He couldn't open the door and jump out, even when Vince slowed around the curves. If he asked to leave the car for any reason, they would follow him with the gun. The gun itself was no longer conveniently placed in the center console where Duncan could reach it if he ever got his hands free. Vince rested the gun in his lap. No, not limited options, no options at all. Duncan would have to wait until they stopped. Perhaps an opportunity would then arise.

He needed to sleep. His eyes felt like two pee holes in the snow. Duncan had never seen pee holes in the snow, having lived his whole life in Miami. He heard the phrase from a kid at school and thought it both hilarious and descriptive. His eyelids drooped every few minutes before snapping open again. He didn't dare let his guard down with Vince and Dorrie. They were ignorant low-lifes, but that didn't mean they weren't dangerous low-lifes. Ignorant and mean can be a bad combination, Duncan now realized.

When they had been on the road for the better part of an hour, Vince pressed the brake and the Toyota slowed to a crawl. "Road's around here somewhere," he said. "Hard to see in the dark."

"You sure about this, Vince?"

"Whaddya mean, *am I sure*? Course I'm sure. Told you the place was secluded."

Just then, Duncan's stomach growled. Dorrie shot a glance over her left shoulder. "Kid's hungry," she said.

"Too bad," Vince said. "He can have one of them granola bars when we get there."

Duncan didn't much care for granola bars but he'd take what he could get and hoped they would arrive before long. The road was deserted. No other cars passed them from either direction. Vince eased along the highway in search of the side road that would lead them to the hidden house of Elvira Applegate. After what seemed an eternity listening to Dorrie's grousing and grumbling, Vince announced they had found the right road. He turned the Toyota hard to the right and up a steep gravel lane. Rocks crunched beneath the tires. In the moonless night, Duncan saw nothing through the windows but a sheet of black. He counted the turns: first right, first left, second right, second left... On the seventh left, a pale glow silhouetted treetops against the horizon.

"There 'tis," Vince said. "The old crow's nest." He stopped the car and handed the gun to Dorrie. "You keep an eye on the kid, while I check the place out." Vince climbed out of the car, coughed three times, spat a big loogie, and lit another Lucky Strike Silver.

Dorrie twisted around and glared at Duncan. "This better work, kid. For all of our sakes. Otherwise, we'll be in the joint and you, well..."

You, well...?

"By the way, what's your name?"

Duncan didn't answer.

"I asked what your name is! You deaf?"

"D-Duncan."

"Duncan what?"

"Duncan Sheets."

"Well, Duncan Sheets, here we is in the middle of nowhere. Absolute, total, complete nowhere. We are in the yah-hahs. No one's gonna find us here. Yes sir, by cracky, old Vince mighta got this one right for a change. Good place to hole up."

They lapsed into silence and Dorrie lit her own umpteenth cigarette, sucking smoke deep into her lungs. Duncan had seen pictures of smoker's lungs during a school health program. *I'll bet these two have lungs like lumps of charcoal. Disgusting, but to my advantage if I can slip away. Gotta stay awake. Gotta stay alert.*

Ten minutes later, Vince jerked open the door of the Highlander. "Okay, we're in. They's a closet upstairs with a key in the lock. We'll put the kid in there. He can't get out. You get us settled. Rustle up some food. We'll toss a few granola bars and water into the closet with the kid. Tomorrow, I'm gonna make *the call*." Vince peered over the back seat of the car. "What's your old man's number?"

Duncan glared at Vince but said nothing.

Vince's face exploded.

He jerked the gun from the top of his trousers and put the barrel right on Duncan's forehead. "I said, what's your old man's number!"

Duncan found himself strangely calm. *No Duncan, no phone number.* He watched with strange fascination as little globs of yellow-white spit formed on Vince's quivering lips. Duncan smiled.

Vince cracked the gun hard against Duncan's skull.

Duncan muffled a cry and held Vince's eyes with his own.

"I can just as easy kill you, kid. I'm in deep enough now. You want to get out of this alive, you best cooperate. You follow?"

Duncan shrugged. A trickle of blood formed on his forehead.

Vince cocked the gun.

"Three–oh–five…" Duncan gave up the number with a raspy voice.

"'At's more like it," Vince said, wiping the spittle from his lips with his tongue. "Now get out."

The gun barrel bored into the nape of Duncan's neck as they walked toward the two-story house looming in the darkness ahead. One pale yard light illuminated the rising walkway. Dorrie followed behind them, wheezing and grunting from the effort she needed to haul herself up the slight incline of the walkway.

Once inside, Vince flipped on several lights.

Despite his grim circumstances, Duncan could see that the old mansion had been restored to its original beauty. Polished hardwood floors gave support for elegant couches and stuffed chairs. A baby grand piano glistened black under the crystal chandelier and pictures of stoic ancestors hung in gilded frames. Plush draperies, elegantly embroidered, cascaded from ceiling to floor framing the many windows now dark against the night sky.

Oddly, Duncan thought about his own rickety house and what it could become with the right kind of remodeling and decorating. *Maybe my mom and dad will remodel without me. They will close up my room and decorate the rest of the house. I won't be around to see it. They'll have another kid to replace me.* He felt the first sting of tears but held them. Vince and Dorrie would never see him snivel.

"Up them stairs," Vince said. "And make it fast."

Duncan trudged up to a landing, made a one-hundred-and-eighty degree pivot, and climbed to the second floor. Coughing, panting and straining to catch his breath, Vince held Duncan in place for a full minute before prodding him down the hallway. When they arrived at a back bedroom, Vince flipped the light switch to reveal soft sage green walls surrounding white wicker furniture. Vince shoved Duncan toward a wooden closet door with a black skeleton key protruding from a hefty deadbolt.

"Get in there," Vince said.

Duncan curled his head around to engage Vince. "What about my hands?"

Vince's mouth sagged into a stupid stare. "Yeah, I guess," Vince said after long moments of sluggish thought. He laid the gun on the bed, pulled out his jackknife, and slit the tape binding Duncan's wrists.

Duncan lunged for the gun.

His hands closed around the grip.

Vince chopped Duncan's wrist with the blade of his hand.

The gun bounced free on the mattress and Vince snatched it from Duncan's reach.

The two stared at one another in ominous silence.

In slow motion, Vince drew the gun to within millimeters of

Duncan's nose. "Into the closet boy."

With a dreadful snick, the closet door shut. The metallic clunk of the deadbolt sealed Duncan in inescapable darkness.

For several minutes, Duncan sat on the floor, rubbed his tender wrists, and waited for his heart rate to slow. He blinked hard. Nothing. Vince had turned off the bedroom light. Not even a thin beam of light leaked around the closet door. Duncan had learned about *total darkness* in an astronomy unit of his science class. The complete absence of light. This had to be it.

He stretched his arms to the side and swept them in a slow arc until his hands met in front of his face. Nothing. He had at least that much space in which to move. He stood slowly and, with his arms to the front, stepped forward. On the second step, his hands touched the wall. *Okay*, he thought to himself. *Now I know how wide this thing is.* He turned ninety degrees to his left and stepped forward again. On the third step, his hands touched what felt like cardboard boxes. *A bit longer than wide.*

As he turned, something slid across his face.

He jumped to the side, crashed into a wall, and waited, his heart pounding.

Seconds slid by. When his heart rate slowed, Duncan raised his hand. Something brushed against his wrist. He froze, eyes wide. He waited. Tightening his courage, he teased the thing with his fingers, then closed his grip. A string. He pulled it. The closet exploded in light. He laughed in relief. A bare bulb shone with blessed brightness in its white porcelain socket. He mumbled a quick prayer of thanksgiving and took a quick inventory of his surroundings.

Elvira Applegate stored her Christmas decorations in the closet. Several boxes of ornaments, greenery, wrapping paper, and garlands were stacked in neat rows at one end of the closet. At the other end, on several wooden shelves were gifts purchased for the Christmas to come. Toys, clothing items, books, and other presents, along with assorted gift receipts, remained sacked and ready for wrapping. Duncan rifled through the sacks. In one, he came upon two D batteries still in their plastic package. Curious, he dug deeper until his hands closed around a cylindrical object. *It couldn't be. Is it? It is!* A flashlight, a beautiful, lovely, God-given yellow flashlight, brand new, and ready for use.

He tore the batteries from the package and inserted them in the flashlight handle. He pushed the switch. Nothing. He unscrewed the top of the flashlight and stared into the battery chamber. *Well duh! Upside down.* He inverted and tried the switch again. A bright beam of light shot from the flashlight. Delighted with his discovery, Duncan whipped the light beam about the room and, for the briefest of moments, forgot his terrible circumstances.

Turning the flashlight off to save the batteries, Duncan began a more thorough investigation of the closet. As his eyes scanned the floor, he noted a brass rim eighteen inches long and raised a fraction of an inch above the wooden floorboards. *A grate? Like the heating grates in my house?* Duncan removed the stack of boxes above the brass rim. *It is! A grate.* He peered through the louvers expecting to see aluminum ductwork. To his surprise, the grate connected to another room on the first floor. From the ceiling light above, he could see shelving in the room below.

As he strained his eyes to examine what lay below the grate, he heard a rattle. Duncan jerked the light string and faded into the closet shadows. Sighs and mumbles wafted through the grate. Dorrie. She recited the names of food. "Chicken noodle soup. Bean soup. Yuck! Spaghetti. Might be good. Canned peaches – nice. Oooh what have we here? A bottle of wine, vino. Yes, yes, that will go nicely with spaghetti and peaches."

The light below winked out, the door shut, and Dorrie was gone.

A pantry. A pantry with a ceiling grate.

EIGHTEEN

The Calls

Each time she wept, Mrs. Sheets knew she could produce no more tears. Yet, every time a new wave of despair engulfed her, her eyes became fountains of anguish. At the moment, her eyes were dry, her mind numb. She sat with her husband on the green couch... waiting. People had been good to them, visiting and praying throughout the day. It was now evening of the first day following Duncan's kidnapping. They had heard nothing from Vincent Puglisi. As each hour passed, they sank further into a deep hole of dread.

A command center for the kidnapping had been set up in the Diamond Police Station. One reserve officer manned the phone and provided a clearinghouse for information and leads. Officers from several jurisdictions had swarmed Dead People's Rejects and the double-wide trailer. They gathered fingerprints, retrieved useful evidence (which wasn't much), and questioned both trailer house neighbors and employees of the antique emporium. The FBI agent coordinated the work of the Evidence Response Team and called for the Child Abduction Rapid Deployment Team from St. Louis. The team was scheduled to arrive at the command center the following day.

Chief Tipton reported the unfortunate news that Vincent Puglisi, and his wife Dorinda, had eluded the police. The Puglisis had made a hasty departure from the trailer house, but law enforcement had no idea where they had gone. This weighed on the minds of Professor and Mrs. Sheets as they waited in the living room of their home.

Now and then, Professor Sheets stood and paced. On one of these short excursions, at 5:01 PM, the shrill ring tone of Professor Sheets' cell phone shattered the somber silence. He started at the sound, came to a complete stop in mid-step, and stared at his phone jangling on the coffee table. The Neosho policeman had gone to his patrol car to take a personal call.

Mrs. Sheets looked at her husband, her brow etched with worry. "Should I go get the officer?" she asked.

"Yes. Hurry. Caller ID says *unknown*," he said. "Hurry!"

Mrs. Sheets ran through the rickety screen door, down the steps, and across the lawn, waving her arms and shouting for the officer to come quickly. The two of them raced back into the house.

Upon entry, they saw Professor Sheets staring at his cell phone. Silence regained the room.

Then a beep.

"Voicemail," Professor Sheets said.

"Play it Delbert," Mrs. Sheets said, a new wave of tears forming in her eyes.

"I'll take it," the officer said. He listened with his eyes closed and his breath held. Twenty seconds later, he lowered the phone and stared at Professor and Mrs. Sheets.

"What?" she said.

"It's him."

"What did he say?"

"The box. You were right. He wants the box. We are to take it to Dead People's Rejects in Blue Eye. We are to go tonight. When he knows the box is in place and nothing has been removed, he will deliver Duncan to us."

"Where?"

"Didn't say."

"That's all he wants… the box?"

"That's what he said."

"So Duncan is okay? He's alive? He's not hurt?"

"He didn't say," the officer said. "I'll call Chief Tipton."

Fifteen minutes later, Chief Biggie Tipton and Sergeant Patsy O'Keefe sat in the front room of the Sheets' house listening to the voice mail on speakerphone.

"Well, we now have it confirmed," Sergeant O'Keefe said. "It's a kidnapping for ransom."

"The box is not important," Professor Sheets said. "Let's just do as he says."

Chief Tipton nodded. "That's exactly what we will do. It is strange that he wants the box put in the antique store. He will know we have heavy surveillance. If he tries to retrieve the box, we'll be all over him. As a part of our surveillance, I want a camera in that office so it can be monitored at all times. I also want pole cameras set up around the place. In addition, I'll check with the FBI."

"Can we go then?" Professor Sheets asked. Urgency filled his words.

"Let me make a few calls and get surveillance operational," Chief Tipton said. "Then we'll be on our way."

A half hour later, Professor Sheets sat in Chief Biggie Tipton's cruiser, Carver's box resting on his lap. The contents of the box had been such an exciting discovery, but now, Professor Sheets couldn't wait to dispense with it. They arrived in Blue Eye at 7:30 PM. Three officers from the Stone County Sheriff's office and a state trooper met them.

"Placed a tiny camera in the office ceiling," a deputy sheriff said. "We're checking it out now. It's trained on the desk so remove as much clutter as possible. Put the box squarely in the center of the desktop. We'll keep officers in unmarked cars nearby, twenty-four-seven. One of them will monitor the camera. All entrances will be under surveillance. He can't get in or out without our spotting him."

"Sounds good," Chief Tipton said.

"Question," one of the state troopers said. "Does it strike you this guy is an idiot? Surely, he can't expect to sneak in here and get that box without being seen."

"I agree," Chief Tipton said. "He's making mistakes, but let's remember, he has pulled off a successful kidnapping and we have no clue where he is. We'll get him but right now the boy is our top priority. We need to rescue him."

The other officers nodded in agreement.

"Since you have this under control," Chief Tipton continued, "we'll be on our way back to Diamond. When the next call comes in, we'll tell him the box is on the desk."

~~~

The second call came minutes before midnight. At 11:47, to be exact. Sergeant Patsy O'Keefe was present when the phone rang.

"Let me take it," she said.

She put the phone on speaker and said, "Hello. This is Sergeant Patricia O'Keefe of the Diamond Police Department."

"Ha!" came the voice through the speaker. "A chick. What's the world comin' to? Woman cops. Pathetic. So, where's the fat guy?"

"If you mean Doctor Delbert Sheets, he is right here listening to you."

"Did you follow my instructions?"

"We did. Now tell us where you plan to release Duncan."

"Is the box in the office at the antique store?"

"Yes. What about the boy?"

"The stuff is still in there? You didn't try nothin' cute like making up fake letters and photo copies didya?"

"Everything is there. No duplicates." Sergeant O'Keefe remained calm but her jaw tightened. "What about the boy Duncan?"

"He's alive."

"When will we get him back?"

The phone clicked to silence.

NINETEEN

Old Timey Alarm Clock

Vince returned from the back yard to the kitchen of Elvira Applegate's house and held his cell phone high above his head. "He done it," he announced to Dorrie who sat at the kitchen table in a threadbare yellow bathrobe filling her face with buttered Saltine crackers.

"Done what?"

"Fat guy put the box back in the office."

"They're gonna nab you, Vince. I can feel it in my bones. By now they'll know what car we got. They'll be watchin' the store like a bunch of turkey vultures. How you gonna get the box without gettin' caught?"

"What you don't know, Dorrie. What nobody but me and Joe Billy Jubal, the owner down in Arkansas, know is this: They's a tunnel. A long tunnel leading from an abandoned storefront a couple of blocks away from the Rejects. Tunnel goes right into the basement of the Rejects. Basement was a speakeasy at one time and that tunnel was how folks snuck into it."

"What's a speakeasy?"

"What's a speakeasy? You don't know what a speakeasy is?"

"If I did, I wouldn'ta asked you, now would I?"

Vince shook his head. "Sometimes your ignorance floors me, Dorrie. Really does. So here's the thing: During Prohibition, when you couldn't sell hooch out in the open, folks fixed up secret places to drink booze what was contraband. Follow?"

"Yeah, I follow. I ain't stupid."

"If you say so. Them secret places for drinking was called speakeasies. In this basement speakeasy under the Rejects, folks went into a neighborhood grocery store what's boarded up now. Then they went down in the basement of that grocery store into the long tunnel. They'd walk through the tunnel to the basement of our little old antique mall and get served up."

Vince reached into his pocket and pulled out a key ring with two keys on it. He jingled them for a few seconds while Dorrie watched with hooded eyes and a mouthful of buttered cracker. "See them keys, Dorrie." He pinched one between his thumb and forefinger. "This one here is to the back door of that old grocery store." Then he pinched the other key. "This one here unlocks the door from the tunnel into the basement."

"How'd you get them?"

"Joe Billy Jubal. He owns the boarded up store too. He give them to me long time back when he first hired me."

"Why?"

"Dunno. Thought I oughta have 'em for some reason, I guess. I ain't told a soul about the tunnel. Got a rug over the trap door to the basement. It's all under wraps."

Dorrie swallowed and licked a smear of butter off her upper lip. "So you get into the office from the tunnel. What if they's a cop sittin' in the office waitin' for you? Then you are a dead duck."

"Maybe not." Vince patted the bulge under his shirt. "I'll be packin'. All nice and legal too. Got a permit. Conceal and carry."

"Kinda don't matter if you got a permit, champ. If you get into a shootout with a cop I mean."

Vince furrowed his brow. "See your point."

"Don't'cha suppose they'll have cameras set up?"

"Probably, but I'll be in and out of the office in a flash. I'll lock the door to the tunnel before they can even storm into the place. It's all good. So, don't worry no more about it, Dorrie. I got it under control. Elvira and her old man left their second car in the garage. Nice one too. Cadillac. I can hotwire it. No one will suspect me in that car. I'll park by the grocery store and watch the place for awhile 'til it feels right to sneak into the tunnel. All goes well, I'll be back here afore sunrise."

"Then what?"

"We hole up for a time then light out for my cousin Lucca's place up by Libby, Montana."

"Libby, Montana. Seriously? That don't sound like Easy Street to me."

"Won't be on Easy Street for a while. I gotta get the letters to that dealer, Ira Badgett. Then we'll get our half mil and hole up."

"I don't want to live in Libby, Montana."

"Won't have to. We'll get some new identities. I know a guy who can fix us up. Licenses, Social Security cards, and the like. Leave it to me. We can live wherever you want."

"Florida. I wanna live in Florida. Naples maybe. Tired of freezin' my bum off. So let's not stay in godforsaken Libby, Montana too long, Vince. Promise me?"

"Yeah. Sure. We'll get to Naples, Florida soon as we can. Vince buttered a cracker and popped it in his mouth. "Gonna leave to get the box in the wee hours of the morning," he said. "Gonna catch forty winks. You see that old timey alarm clock up there by the bed?"

"Yeah. What about it?"

"Betcha that thing'll wake the dead. Gonna set it for 4:00 AM. Then ole Vince is off to Blue Eye in the old crow's Caddie."

"What about the kid?"

"Not sure yet. Might just leave him here. Might drop him somewhere. Might whack him. That might be the best option. He can identify us."

"I don't favor killin' the kid, Vince. Let's just drop him off somewhere."

"Don't go soft on me now Dorrie. Or they's no Easy Street."

"Whatever you say, Vince. Whatever you say."

TWENTY

Stuck

After discovery of the grate that first night, Duncan slept fitfully, until waking to the faint sound of birds in the trees. *Must be morning.* As he raised his arms to stretch, the deadbolt rattled. He held his breath. The door swung open. Vince loomed in the doorway with two power bars, a bottle of water, and a Styrofoam bowl filled with canned peaches.

"Here," Vince said, placing the food on the floor as if Duncan were a dog. He slammed the closet door and locked it, plunging Duncan into darkness once again. When Vince's footsteps faded, Duncan switched on his flashlight, slid down the closet wall, and snatched the plastic spoon protruding from the Styrofoam bowl. He wolfed down the peaches and one of the power bars before taking a long drag on the water.

In late morning, Vince unlocked the door again and let Duncan out to relieve himself by marching him at gunpoint to the upstairs bathroom. Before, re-imprisoning him, Vince pushed another power bar and bottle of water into Duncan's stomach. Fearing this might be the last food he would receive that day, he reserved the power bar and drank sparingly from the bottle of water.

Twenty minutes later, after listening with his ears pricked,

Duncan satisfied himself that Vince had vacated the second floor. He switched on the overhead light and crawled to the grate. Careful to keep silence, he inserted the handle of the plastic spoon under the rim of the grate. To his relief, no fasteners held the grate and, within seconds, he had extracted it from the floor.

Lowering his head through the opening in the floor, Duncan shone the flashlight into the room below. The fully stocked pantry shelves extended from floor to ceiling and one bank of shelves rose to within a foot from the grate. "Excellent," he whispered to himself. "Once through the opening, I can climb down the shelves, ease out the pantry door, and scoot."

He trained the flashlight beam on the pantry door and nodded when he saw it latched with a simple doorknob. No locks. No deadbolts. *Tonight. After Vince and Dorrie have hit the sack, I'll slip through the opening...I hope. Looks a bit narrow for me. I wish I was Tina. She could drop through the opening without hitting the sides!* With his plan formed, Duncan replaced the grate and began his long vigil until nightfall.

Time passed with agonizing slowness and Duncan ran the plan through his mind over again. There were several critical considerations. First would be slipping through the grate opening. Then he would have to climb down the shelves without knocking anything off and making a disastrous noise. Of course, escaping the house could be tricky if either Vince or Dorrie slept lightly. Once out of the house, he had no idea where to go. He could go down the seven-curve lane to the highway. However, if Vince or Dorrie discovered his escape, they would surely follow the same course. And where did the highway go? Which direction should he take?

Since they had arrived at Elvira Applegate's house by night, he had no knowledge of the countryside. That could be a huge problem in the dark if he decided to veer off the roadways into dense forest. And what would he encounter in the forest? Were there neighbors in the vicinity? Would they even open their doors to him in the middle of the night? Yes, there were lots of considerations and, as his mind raced through them, his stomach tightened into a hard little knot.

A knot's in one's stomach and time on one's hands, can bring on prayer, or so Duncan discovered as he sat on the closet floor, waiting. He had never spent extended time praying. Of course, he said grace at mealtimes and joined his parents for bedtime prayers, but while alone, he rarely prayed. This time, however, with a dangerous operation ahead of him, Duncan found himself asking God for protection. He remembered the minister in his new church telling the congregation, "You should pray for exactly what you desire. Be specific." So Duncan asked God to help him through the grate opening, down the shelves – quietly – and out of the house. He prayed that Vince and Dorrie would sleep so soundly they would not discover his escape until hours after he had gone. He also prayed for a car to spot him on the highway, preferably a state highway patrolman.

It must have been evening when Vince unlocked the door and peered at Duncan sitting on the floor of the closet. "I called your old man tonight," he said. "Told him to put that box you stole back where you found it. If he does that I aim to let you go. I'm going to call again in a few minutes. See if he done what he was told."

"You'll never get away with it," Duncan said.

"We'll see about that hotshot. You better hope your old man puts the box back. If not, it ain't goin' to go well for you. Follow?"

Duncan swallowed hard and nodded. *Dad will put the box back. I know that. Still, I'm not taking any chances. I gotta get out of here tonight.* For the next several hours, he arranged and rearranged the power bar and water near the edge of the grate. Once through the grate, he would reach up and retrieve them, then down the shelves. Tricky, for sure, but he had always prided himself in being sure-footed, slow but sure-footed.

He heard no more from Vince that night. After an estimated two, perhaps three more hours, when the last sounds in the house died, the moment for escape had come.

Duncan removed the grate, rearranged the water and power bars for the last time, and switched on the flashlight.

Lowering his legs through the opening, he eased downward until his feet hit the top shelf. With the toes of his sneakers, he pushed several boxes and jars to the back of the shelf to give himself solid footing. He dropped a few more inches until only his arms, shoulders, neck, and head remained upstairs in the closet. Then he took a deep breath and raised his arms, hoping to slip the rest of the way into the pantry. He dropped an inch, no more. To his horror, the grate opening grabbed him as if he were gripped in a vise. He couldn't go up or down. Duncan Sheets had wedged himself so tightly in the grate opening that he could not move.

Just then, the shrill sound of an old timey alarm clock shattered the silence of Elvira Applegate's house.

He couldn't go up or down.

TWENTY-ONE

Tunnel

Vince did a fine job of stinking up Elvira Applegate's new Cadillac with smoke from the eight cigarettes he inhaled, one after another, on his return to Blue Eye. He drove the speed limit, taking thirty minutes to reach a side street that offered him a good view of Dead People's Rejects. He killed the engine extinguished his headlights. *Okay. Let's see what's happening.* He lit a Lucky Strike Silver, slid down in the seat, lowered the bill of his red Philadelphia Phillies cap, and began surveillance of the antique mall.

He spotted two cars, one black, one dark blue, positioned to give those inside a good three hundred and sixty degree view of the Rejects. *So there you are boys – or maybe girls. What's this world comin' to? Chick cops. Whatever. Got you spotted. Yessir. I not only got a light, I got a box, and I got a half a mil just waitin' to heat up my wallet. So keep an eye out coppers. I'm about to slip right under your nose. Watch this.*

With the headlights off, Vince eased the Cadillac down the side street to a position behind the old grocery store. The police in the unmarked cars could not see him from their vantage point near the antique mall. He waited fifteen minutes to be sure no one came around the corner to check on him. He scanned the buildings in the vicinity. Most were abandoned and in disrepair. An old but well-maintained single-story house was in eyeshot but Vince doubted if anyone were awake inside since the windows were dark and the shades pulled. His confidence brimmed. No one had spotted him. He took a last drag on his cigarette, stubbed it in the ashtray, and slipped out of the Cadillac, door key in hand.

Once inside the grocery store, his high-intensity flashlight beam found a path to the basement door. Old shelving, an antique brass cash register, and boxes of canned goods, decades past their expiration date, cluttered the basement floor. The door to the tunnel hung askew on one hinge. Vince pulled the door aside and directed his light beam into the tunnel. A thick white electrical wire hung from beams set on ancient oak four-by-fours coursing the length of the tunnel. "Had lights at one time," Vince said under his breath. "Lighting the way to white lightning." He snickered to himself, pleased with his clever word play.

As he made his way along the tunnel, he held the flashlight before him to clear the way of elegant cobwebs engineered by assorted arachnids. Now and then a clod of dry dirt followed by a stream of soil particles fell to the tunnel floor. When he reached the door to the antique store, he put the flashlight in his mouth and focused the beam on a large padlock. He inserted the second key and with a quick snick of the lock, opened the door and entered the confines of a once carefree and raucous speakeasy.

~~~

Sergeant William "Porky" Snodgrass and Corporal Wiley Higgins waited in their unmarked car, eyes glued to a small monitor attached to the dashboard. The image on the screen had remained unchanged for the span of their surveillance. They had been on duty for nearly eight hours and looked forward to the end of their shift.

"Stakeouts like these numb my mind," Porky said.

"Numb my bum," Wiley said, shifting in his seat and squeaking his thick leather belt. He glanced up to survey the area around the antique mall, squinting at the other unmarked car. Nothing moved. "Sure is quiet," he said.

"Doesn't look like anything's going down tonight. Can't wait to get off. I'm heading to Belle's for a giant breakfast – eggs, biscuits and red eye gravy, and at least four cups of steaming hot coffee. Probably some extra crunchy hashbrowns." He burped in anticipation.

Suddenly, Wiley shot into a full upright position, eyes wide, the hairs on the back of his neck bristling. "Pork! Look."

A hand reached for the box. Just as quickly the hand disappeared. Porky snatched the microphone and barked an alert to his fellow officers who poured out of their vehicles in a full sprint to the Rejects. Weapons drawn and flashlights ablaze they covered one another as they entered the store.

Porky Snodgrass entered the office first and, noting the strewn scatter rug, pointed to the trap door. With officers ringing the trap door, weapons drawn, Porky jerked the handle of the trap door. The officers pointed flashlight beams into the basement from each side of the opening. Once satisfied that the basement was clear, the four officers scuttled down the steps. Porky grasped the knob of the tunnel door and pulled hard, to no avail.

"Locked," he said and holstered his firearm.

TWENTY-TWO

Peanut Oil

Duncan dangled. For long minutes, Duncan dangled. The clanging alarm clock had finally stopped and he could hear Vince coughing and struggling to raise gobs of nighttime crud from lungs. Duncan whispered to himself, "What if he checks on me? What if he comes into the pantry?" Minutes later, the roar of an engine in the garage brought a wave of relief. *He's leaving. To Blue Eye?*

While Dorrie slept, Duncan returned to his predicament. For some reason, divine intervention, perhaps, he recalled a discussion in his health class. They had been studying human respiration. He remembered the term *vital capacity*, which his textbook had defined as *the maximum amount of air a person can expel after taking a maximum inhalation*. He knew that if he expelled the air in his vital capacity, his rib cage would narrow. *Might be just enough to get unstuck!*

Duncan put his feet on the top shelf, sucked in a deep breath, and blew out all the air he could. Then, red faced, he held his breath and gave a mighty push with his feet. Two inches! He raised himself two full inches. It was just enough to gain leverage with his arms on the floor of the closet. Pushing with his arms and feet, he liberated himself from the grate opening.

He sat on the floor cross-legged, catching his breath. *Now what?*

After resting several seconds to lower his heart rate, he lowered his head through the grate opening. His flashlight beam fixed on a bottle resting on the top shelf. He had noticed it when he had pushed items back on that shelf to give his feet room. But, in his haste he had paid scant attention. The bottle contained a clear yellowish oil, and the label read, *Dr. George Washington Carver's Peanut Rubbing Oil, Relieves Minor Aches and Pains, 4 oz.* Duncan grabbed it.

Back in the closet, he unscrewed the lid of the jar, sniffed it, and put his finger into the oil. He rubbed a drop between his thumb and forefinger. *Slippery. Might just work.* He stripped off his shirt and dropped it through the opening. Then with generous portions of George Washington Carver's Peanut Rubbing Oil, he greased his chest, arms, shoulders, and as much of his back as he could reach. *I wish I was Tina. She's so skinny she could probably reach around and oil her entire back!*

Three minutes later, satisfied that he was as slimy as he could get, he stuffed the power bar in his pants pocket and took a deep breath. He blew out his vital capacity and lowered himself through the grate opening.

Schloop.

He slipped right through and caught himself by his hands on the rim of the opening. He paused to smile at his own ingenuity, then grabbed the bottle of water and flashlight. Down the shelves he went. Nothing toppled. *So far, so good.* Without bothering to button it, the tugged his shirt over his oily torso. He killed the flashlight and padded to the pantry door, thankful for his "squeakless" sneakers.

Duncan took an entire minute to rotate the doorknob. With the latch freed, he cracked the door. To his horror, it emitted a long, slow squeal. He froze. Ears pricked, he listened for Dorrie. After several long, agonizing seconds, hearing nothing, he jerked the door. Another squeal, sharp this time but short. He stood statue still, listening.

Nothing.

He took a deep breath, stuck his head into the hallway and completed a quick flashlight scan of the rooms. To his immediate right, he saw a kitchen with a mudroom beyond leading through a back door to the yard. With the flashlight off, he tiptoed through the darkness toward the kitchen. He fixed his eyes on the pale glow from the yard light streaming through the window of the back door. Suddenly, his leg hit a chair toppling it to the floor with a loud clatter. *O great! That'll wake Dorrie for sure!* He raced to the mudroom and plastered himself against the wall.

He waited.

To his amazed relief, Dorrie did not appear. *Now!* He eased the door open and scurried into the back yard. Quickly, he rounded the house and stared into the distance. The curvy lane appeared to be his only option because the woods around the house were thick and impenetrable. He considered his next move.

Just then, he felt something. If the truth be told, he didn't *feel* anything. Not really. Nor did he see anything. He simply sensed it and jerked himself to the left just as something whished by his shoulder. Dorrie embedded the tip of a fireplace poker deep in the sod. She grunted cursed under her breath as she struggled to free the poker. Unable to do so, she lunged at Duncan and grabbed the tail of his unbuttoned shirt. It slipped easily from his body. Duncan pitched the water bottle at Dorrie's head and took off on a sprint, far exceeding his top speed of *slow.*

He switched on his flashlight and began the zigzag course down the lane toward the highway. Just as he rounded the third curve he heard an ear-shattering shot followed by a spray of buckshot into the surrounding trees and bushes. *A shotgun! She has a shotgun! Where did that come from?*

Duncan dropped to a crouch and dashed into the thick underbrush as another volley of buckshot peppered the surrounding foliage. Recognizing that the light beam was her target, Duncan switched off his flashlight and plowed through the bushes, clawing at the branches that scratched and ensnared him. He fell multiple times but heaved himself to his feet and scrambled on. After five minutes of clawing through the brush, he stopped, exhausted, and put his hands on his knees. He sucked in deep breaths and waited, hidden behind a large oak tree.

Headlights wove through the curves of the lane and stopped at the point where Duncan had entered the tangled forest. In the distance, he saw Dorrie open the door of the Toyota Highlander and pull the shotgun from the passenger seat.

"I know you is in there," she shouted. "You move and make a sound, I'm gonna fire. My daddy taught me to shoot and I ain't forgot how. Makes no never mind to me and Vince, you get plugged now rather than later. No never mind 't all."

Duncan said nothing.

"Got you pinned down, kid. Got all the time in the world. Come daybreak, I'm gonna get you. Might look up."

Instinctively, Duncan raised his eyes and through the tree tops he glimpsed the graying of an early morning sky. It wouldn't be long before she could track him through the broken underbrush. He doubted that she could move rapidly, given her bulk, but Duncan knew desperate people can do amazing things. He knew Dorrie would fire away as soon as she got a glimpse of him. Even through thick foliage, the buckshot could hit its mark – Duncan Carl Sheets.

TWENTY-THREE

Joe Billy Jubal

Wheezing like a freight train, Vince raced through the tunnel. When he emerged from its narrow confines, he took several seconds to cough up the pent-up phlegm from deep in his lungs. He spat a gob on the dusty floor. *'Bout got this one licked. A few more minutes and I'll be on the road to Easy Street.* He switched off his flashlight and ascended the stairs to the back room of the store. Cracking the door a sliver, he peered into the alleyway. Nothing. *Ha! Home free!*

No sooner had he stepped from the threshold of the back door than a dozen high-beam flashlights exploded in his face.

"Freeze!" A voice from the blinding light. "Very slowly, put the box on the ground, and put your hands in the air."

With one arm raised, Vince lowered the box to the graveled alley. One officer snatched the pistol from his waistband as another cuffed his hands behind his back. Porky Snodgrass screeched to a stop, jumped from his cruiser, and strode toward Vince.

"Vincent Puglisi," Porky intoned, "you are under arrest for kidnapping and extortion. You have the right to remain silent. Anything you say can and may be used against you in a court of law. Yada, yada, yada. Do you understand these rights as I have read them to you?"

Vince nodded. "Not saying a word."

"Your choice," Porky said and led Vince to one of the parked squad cars.

Vince glanced to his left. A man with curly gray hair leaned against his car, arms folded across his chest.

"Ah nuts!" Vince said. "That's Joe Billy Jubal. You found Joe Billy Jubal."

"That we did," Porky said. "Told us all about the tunnel so we could set a trap for you. We weren't sure you would use the tunnel, but in case you did, we had you covered. See that house over there? You looked straight at it a few minutes ago. These officers were in that house, ready and waiting."

Vince shook his head in disgust and fell into the back seat of the squad car.

Joe Billy Jubal waved goodbye.

TWENTY-FOUR

Skunk Hole

Duncan lowered himself to the ground behind the large oak tree making himself as small as possible. Without a shirt, he had become a picnic ground for mosquitoes and chiggers, probably ticks too. The forest rested in silence. Through the trees, Duncan saw the headlights of the Toyota. He couldn't see Dorrie but imagined her leaning against the hood of the van, smoking cigarettes... waiting.

Duncan tried to formulate a plan. He had to get to the highway where he could flag an oncoming car. But, the highway meant exposure and Dorrie could run him down, shoot him, or both. Frenzied mosquitoes swarmed him. No wonder! Several deeper branch scratches oozed droplets of blood. *I need a little help here, God.*

"Good mornin'. Gettin' lighter. I know right where you is!" Dorrie shouted, her voice lilting, mocking. Duncan's skin puckered in goose bumps.

"Boom!" Dorrie shouted with a menacing cackle.

That did it. Duncan leapt to his feet, and sprinted deeper into the hardwood jungle.

A spray of buckshot slammed against bark, branch, and leaf,

just above his head. A pellet hit him in the shoulder. He stifled a cry and veered to the left, zig-zagging as he went. Dorrie thundered after him. Even in the throes of his panic, he was amazed that this flabby old woman could move with such alarming speed. Two nights ago she could barely haul herself up the incline from the van to Elvira Applegate's house. Sometimes desperate people can do amazing things. His shoulders hunched in anticipation of another blast of buckshot.

Where is the highway! Should have reached it by now!

He scuttled on. A quick left. Then a quick right.

Boom!

Boom!

Both shots missed.

Duncan dropped to a crouch and powered through the underbrush.

Suddenly, his left foot plunged into a skunk hole. Something snapped and a bolt of pain shot through his leg. He collapsed to the ground, groaning in agony. Excruciating. *Must have broken it.* He tried to stand but tumbled back to the ground. His foot looked kinked, at the wrong angle. His heart pulsed in his throat. He took two deep breaths. *Gotta keep moving.* He turned and hoisted himself to his knees. With his injured foot raised above the ground, he took several tentative steps on all fours. He stopped. All quiet.

Then it happened.

Cold steel ground into the back of his neck.

"Hello, kid. Top of the mornin' to you." Dorrie's words settled upon him like sacks of frozen peas. "Up. Stand up."

"I can't. My foot's hurt."

"Tough. Get up. I ain't carrying you back to the van and Vince will be here afore long. So get up."

Duncan grasped a low tree branch and hauled himself to a standing position on his right foot. As he did so, he saw a soft carpet of leaves trailing into the distance. Dorrie had sneaked up on him by tiptoeing along that leaf-lined trail he had somehow missed in his frenzy to escape.

"Move!"

Dorrie marched Duncan in a tortured hobble back to the van where she made him lie on the ground. With the shotgun cradled on her left forearm, she single-handedly lit a cigarette and took several deep drags. The gravel from the lane poked his lacerated chest. He could smell the earthy roadbed beneath his face and shivered in the morning chill. His escape had failed. Tears formed, but he sniffed and shook his head. Dorrie would not see him cry.

His ankle throbbed, swelling in his sneaker.

A mosquito whined in his ears.

He braced for the bite but it never happened. He could still hear the whine but felt no stinger.

Duncan's brow furrowed.

Not a mosquito?

No? A siren? Maybe a siren?

A siren! More than one siren!

Louder. Closer.

"Oh no!" Dorrie said and emitted a string of curses far beyond anything Duncan had ever heard on the playground or in his school locker room.

"Thank you, God," he whispered to the rocks beneath his face. "Thank you."

PART THREE

TWENTY-FIVE

The Ceremony

November can be iffy in southwest Missouri but on this day, the weather cooperated. Three weeks had passed since Professor and Mrs. Sheets received that blessed phone call and heard the crackling words, "Folks, we have him. He's safe …all scratched and chigger bit. Might have a broken foot. The ambulance is on its way. They'll take him to the hospital in Branson if you want to head there to meet the ambulance. The Puglisis are in custody. Turns out there is another perp. Fellow by the name of Lewis Crabtree. Officers are picking him up as we speak. You want to talk to Duncan? He's sitting here munching a power bar." Neither Professor nor Mrs. Sheets had ever heard happier words than, "Hi Mom. Hi Dad. Boy, have I got a story to tell you."

And that's just what Duncan prepared to do as the sun warmed a murmuring crowd gathered outside the George Washington Carver National Monument. The trees had shed their leaves, signaling the near onset of winter. But on this day, light jackets and sweaters kept dignitaries and guests comfortable as they waited upon folding chairs. Four-dozen people, give or take a few, were in attendance. Important visitors included Congressman Will Miller; several local legislators; Doctor Philo Peacock, a history professor who traveled all the way from Tuskegee Institute; and the usual assortment of local civic leaders. Correspondents and cameramen from three Springfield television stations roamed the lawn filming and conducting interviews. The CBS affiliate from Kansas City also made an appearance virtually guaranteeing national exposure.

Following Gideon's invocation, Monument Superintendent Frank Calloway officially received the letters and artifacts contained in Carver's Box. He explained the historical significance of the Jamison Collection, described how the documents would be preserved and protected, and thanked the family for its generosity. On a side table, five of the letters, including the first, were in a glass display case.

Earlier, copies of the letters had been given to Professor Sheets for his historical research. He already had two papers submitted for publication. One carried the title, *The Significance of the Jamison Collection in Understanding the Educational Development of George Washington Carver.* The other had been titled, *New Evidence in the Disappearance of Industrialist Rudolf Diesel.* Duncan had tried to read the papers, but as might be expected, Professor Sheets took simple ideas and made them quite complex with big words and fancy sentences.

Having completed his prepared remarks, Superintendent Calloway motioned Duncan forward. Now proficient in using crutches, Duncan poled himself to the podium. With his hand on Duncan's shoulder, the superintendent leaned into the microphone. "Ladies and gentlemen, before we break for refreshments, I wish to introduce to you this young man. He has been through quite an ordeal regarding these wonderful letters. His name is Duncan Sheets. I'll let him tell his story."

Duncan had never spoken to so many and he certainly had never been filmed or interviewed by reporters. Butterflies whiffled his stomach and his tongue dried up like a block of Styrofoam. He looked over at Professor Sheets who gave a quick flick of his mustache. This was a pre-arranged signal from father to son that sent the message: *You are well prepared. We've practiced it plenty of times. Once you've been in Elvira Applegate's closet, the rest is a walk in the park.*

Before beginning his speech, Duncan beckoned Tina to join him at the podium. She scowled, pursed her lips, and shook her head in refusal, causing a twitter of laughter from the crowd. Duncan insisted and a gentle nudge from Marty Ng sent her on a brisk walk to the podium. She crossed her arms over her chest and did a little body twist to relieve her nerves.

Duncan lowered the microphone, cleared his throat, and told the story of how he and Tina had found, lost, and retrieved the box. Reporters scribbled furiously to memorialize what later became known as the *Bunny-Suit Caper*. Increasing in confidence and with a stronger voice, Duncan explained how he had joined Tina and his parents in a systematic study of the letters. He remembered to include several sentences on Rudolf Diesel and his connection to Doctor Carver.

Silence enveloped the audience as Duncan recounted his imprisonment in Elvira Applegate's closet. Elivra, by the way, sat perched on the edge of her front-row seat. After describing his ill-fated attempt to wedge through the grate opening, he reached under into his pocket and fished out a jar of George Washington Carver's Peanut Oil. He placed it atop the podium. "This oil is for muscle aches and pains. Mrs. Applegate had two bottles on a top shelf in her pantry. I could reach them from the attic. After I got stuck, I took off my shirt, greased up with peanut oil, and down I went."

The audience howled with laughter.

As the last giggles faded, Duncan held a sheet of paper high in the air for all to see. "This is one of the Jamison letters," he said. "I'd like to read a section to you." Placing the letter on the podium, he read:

My dear Jenny,

Thank you so much for your recent letter and the sweet sentiments contained therein. Most of my time is now spent with <u>our</u> patients. I underline the word <u>our</u>, because I can feel your prayers for these many sufferers who come to me. God speaks through these peanut oils in marvelous ways. The massages I administer are bringing great relief. Just the other day a small girl, five or six years old, walked up to me and gave me the biggest hug. Two months prior, she could not walk and her parents carried her into my office. Daily *treatment with peanut oil has restored her ability to walk. You will remember that beautiful short verse from Philippians, chapter four, verse thirteen,* I can do all things through Christ, which strengtheneth me. *That is how I feel. Christ is working through me and through these precious oils that He has put before us for our use and His glory.*

Duncan set the letter down and scanned the audience. "I'll bet," he continued, "that George Washington Carver never dreamed his oils would be used to grease a kid for an escape. Looks like God still uses peanut oil."

The people roared with laughter again and shot to their feet in a standing ovation. Duncan picked up his jar of peanut oil and walked back to his beaming parents.

The crowd mingled for a time, perusing the letters, chatting with Duncan and his parents, and enjoying refreshments. As the crowd began to dissipate, an elderly white-haired gentleman approached the Sheets family. He removed his green alpine hat, smoothed a hatband feather, and stooped to extend his hand in greeting.

"Hello," he said with a thick German accent. "My name is Otto Vogel. I am from Saint Louis and I am a distant relative, by marriage, of Rudolf Diesel. A woman named Lucy Lucier, a private investigator, contacted one of Rudolf's relatives in Germany and explained this discovery of yours. That relative called me and asked if I might attend this ceremony and obtain a copy of the letter from Rudolf."

Professor Sheets seized this opportunity to speak to Otto Vogel in German. After several seconds of what seemed incomprehensible gibberish, Duncan and Tina scurried off in search of a remaining chocolate chip cookie.

TWENTY-SIX

Red Paper Package

Magical. Totally awesome, magical, freaky, wonderful, Duncan thought to himself as he stared out the picture window at cotton-ball snowflakes floating before his eyes. Evening was at hand. Duncan's first snowflakes drifted from the heavens above into the bright beam of the porch light before slipping out of sight. He had become so entranced that his parents excused him from helping them decorate the Christmas tree.

The doorbell rang and Duncan, now free of crutches, raced to the door. The Ng family stood before him brushing the snow from their caps and coats. To Duncan's surprise, Tina and her parents had been joined by a tall slim girl of sixteen. Shiny black hair protruded from beneath her gray stocking cap. She sported two small gold-ball earrings, nothing more, and bore a smile so wide it thinned her eyes.

"Come in. Come in," Professor Sheets shouted from behind his son. "Duncan, where are your manners?"

As the Ngs came into the front room, Mrs. Sheets extended her hand to the older daughter, "And you must be Tonya. Welcome. It is nice to meet you."

Shyly, Tonya took Mrs. Sheets' hand as Professor Sheets and

CARVER'S BOX

Duncan grabbed coats, hats, and scarves from the visitors and took them to the hall closet.

With the snowstorm described with insightful phrases such as, *a big one, lots of accumulation,* and *keeping the plows busy,* all gathered in the living room. Tina sat next to her sister on the floor, their shoulders touching. Both girls wore black leggings, red dresses, and identical gold cross necklaces.

"What pretty cross necklaces you have…," Mrs. Sheets said. Her voice trailed, inviting an explanation as to why two unbelieving girls would wear a symbol of Christ's sacrifice and victory.

Tonya accepted the invitation. "When I was in rehab, I became a believer. In fact, I could not have survived nor gotten well had it not been for my new faith. It was pretty rough for the first few weeks in Tulsa, but then one of the counselors spoke of her faith. I resisted her message at first but she was patient, not pushy, not giving up either. One night, after an extremely tough time, I lay in my bed and prayed for the first time. A wave of peace rolled over me and, as they say, *the rest is history.*" Her wide, eye-thinning smile reappeared. "Here I am, clean and free. That counselor gave me this necklace as I was leaving to come home."

Mrs. Sheets smiled. Professor Sheets nodded. Duncan blurted, "But what about you Tina. Why do you have a cross necklace?"

Tina puckered her face and stuck her tongue out at Duncan. "I already told you my sister is a genius. If she believes in this stuff then so do I because I'm a genius too. So there! Satisfied?"

Duncan suppressed a smile and nodded, shooting a glance toward his parents both of whom were also suppressing smiles.

"We want to go to church with you," Tonya said.

"That would be fine if it's all right with your parents," Professor Sheets said.

"It's okay," Mr. Ng said. "My wife and I won't go. We're not there yet. But if the girls wish to go, we won't stand in their way."

The conversation lulled and Mr. Ng lifted a package from a paper sack he had been carrying. "Tonya has something for you." He handed the red-paper package to Tonya who gave it to Professor Sheets.

"What is this?" Professor Sheets asked.

"You'll see," Tonya said.

151

Professor Sheets. "Am I to open this?"

"Please do," Mr. Ng said.

Carefully, Professor Sheets peeled the gold ribbon and red tissue paper from its contents. He withdrew a black wallet, cracked with age. He looked at Tonya. "Is this…?

"Go ahead and open it," she said.

Professor Sheets unbuckled the wallet strap. He peeled apart the soft leather covers to reveal a check made out to Professor Sheets for sixteen thousand dollars. His jaw dropped. "What is this?"

"It is the repayment of a loan," Marty Ng said. "My wife Ming had discovered the wallet after the kids hid the box in our barn. She had the bills appraised. Some were worth more than their face value. The ten thousand dollars contained in the wallet were worth more like fifteen thousand. We used the money for Tonya's treatment. I had just lost my job, and we had no money to pay for the inpatient care she received. We didn't handle this properly but I couldn't get a loan because I was unemployed. We were desperate. Tonya had to be saved. Now that I'm back working, I received a short-term loan to pay you back. We added a thousand dollars to pay for the inconvenience and worry we caused you. Consider it interest on the loan." Marty Ng hung his head. "I am sorry for borrowing the money without your permission. I didn't know what else to do."

Silence descended on the room for several long seconds.

"Well," Professor Sheets said, flicking his mustache three times. "I imagine Doctor Carver would have considered Tonya's care to be a fine use for this money. Do you know how that sum of money came into Jenny Jamison's hands?"

The Ngs shook their heads in unison.

"Doctor Carver lived a simple life. He often failed to cash his paychecks because he didn't need the money. We found a letter to Jenny Jamison from the early 1920s. In this letter, Doctor Carver said he would, from time-to-time send her money. We think the money found in that black wallet came from him."

"Why did he send the money to her," Marty Ng asked.

Professor Sheets shrugged. "Don't know for sure. Perhaps he thought Jenny had no reliable source of income and wanted to help her out. I doubt we will ever know." Professor Sheets paused and flicked his mustache again – the customary three times. "I have an idea," he said. "We don't need this money. Why don't we set up the George Washington Carver Scholarship Fund and use the proceeds to help a graduate of Diamond High School who wants to attend college?"

"I think that's a great idea," Mr. Ng said.

Tina twisted her lips to the side. "So we're not going to spend it?"

"Not for ourselves," Mr. Ng said.

"That's really dumb," Tina said crossing her arms in an obvious harrumph.

Laughter followed.

Mrs. Sheets stood from her chair and clapped her hands together. "How about coffee for the adults," Mrs. Sheets said. "And I think we have lime Kool Aid. Maybe some Oreos."

"Double stuffed?" Tina asked.

"Of course."

They traipsed behind Mrs. Sheets to the kitchen.

Tina leaned toward Duncan and whispered, "Not spending the money. Dumb. Really dumb. But guess what? I will win the scholarship. You just wait and see, Dunk Sheets."

The End

QUESTIONS AND WORDS

Some Questions to Ponder
(Don't read ahead in the story or the ending won't be a surprise.)

1. What words or phrases would you use to describe the following characters?
   Duncan
   Tina
   Professor Sheets
   Mrs. Sheets
   Vincent Puglisi
   Dorinda Puglisi
   Large Lewis Crabtree

2. What do you think Duncan and Tina should have done with the $10,000 when they first discovered the money?

3. Why do you think the author included the scene on making gummy candy?

4. Were you surprised that Tina admitted her role in breaking into the basement? Why or why not? Why do you think she cried when she made this admission?

5. Should Professor Sheets and Mister Ng have called the police and abandoned their own search for the box? Why or why not?

6. Did Isaac Beiler have the right to sell the box? Why or why not? Did the antique dealer have the right to buy it? Why or why not?

7. What do you think of the Amish view that modern technology can draw people away from devotion to God?

8. Doctor Carver felt nature brought him closer to God. Can you describe a time when you felt closer to God through nature?

9. Did the Sheets/Ng Investigative Agency have the right to buy back the box from the antique dealer? Why or why not? Should

they have called the police when they discovered the box in Dead People's Rejects? Why or why not?

10. Duncan wondered if his memory of studying vital capacity in health class was divine intervention (God giving him the memory). What do you think?

11. Why do you think the author included the story about Rudolf Diesel (a story within a story)?

12. Was it acceptable for the Ngs to "borrow" the money in the wallet? Why or why not?

13. What are the three most important indications that God was present in this story?

A Few Words for the Dictionary

(The chapter in which the word appears is in parentheses.)

1. agitation (3)
2. barmy (9)
3. biodiesel (11)
4. blue-haired (6)
5. careen (13)
6. conspiratorial (6)
7. decompose (9)
8. dilapidated (3)
9. dispense (18)
10. dissipate (25)
11. downsize (8)
12. embed (23)
13. excruciating (24)
14. gander (10)
15. horticulture (13)
16. illumine (17)
17. indignation (17)
18. jostle (6)
19. lacerate (24)
20. legion (15)
21. leverage (22)
22. lumen (2)
23. lyrics (9)
24. mannequin (7)
25. micromanage (12)
26. morph (6)
27. mote (3)
28. muster (6)
29. obscurity (12)

30. peruse (25)
31. pickaninny (7)
32. proficient (25)
33. pugnacious (1)
34. raucous (21)
35. sarcastic (1)
36. squelch (14)
37. stoic (17)
38. trove (3)
39. vacate (20)
40. writhe (9)

Author's Note

When each of my grandchildren enters her/his eighth year of life, I write a novel. *Carver's Box* was especially written for and dedicated to my grandson Flint. He has an abiding interest in science and is also a boy devoted to God. Some months before I began writing *Carver's Box*, his grandmother and I took him to visit the George Washington Carver National Monument in Diamond, Missouri. He is also a big fan of the Hardy Boys books, preferring the older volumes to the newer. These factors, science, God, the GWC National Monument, and mystery formed the elements for this story.

It is a work of historical fiction. The broad elements of George Washington Carver's life presented in the novel are accurate as are the essentials of Rudolf Diesel's work and mysterious death on a voyage across the English Channel. The Carver Monument is located near Diamond, Missouri and Neosho's Crowder College is an important educational institution in the state of Missouri. A significant body of Carver's correspondence is preserved and the letters to Jenny Jamison, a fictitious character, do follow Carver's style of writing at various points in his life. One can still buy Doctor George Washington Carver's Peanut Oil in two-ounce and four-ounce bottles as well as spray cans.

A number of people deserve my heartfelt thanks. In particular, I wish to thank Lieutenant Justin Arnold and Captain Tim Clothier of the Ozark, Missouri Police Department who provided such excellent counsel on police procedure. Of course, my best editor and critic, as always has been my wife Jean Ann.

www.ingramcontent.com/pod-product-compliance
Lightning Source LLC
Chambersburg PA
CBHW070329130626
46556CB00007B/2775